Mad Dog Goes to Hollywood

Mad Dog Goes to Hollywood

A
Novel
by
Dennis Perry
with
Everett 'Mad Dog' Perry

Mad Dog Goes to Hollywood

iUniverse books may be ordered through booksellers or by contacting:

iUniverse
1663 Liberty Drive
Bloomington, IN 47403
www.iuniverse.com
1-800-Authors (1-800-288-4677)

ISBN: 978-1-4917-9900-0
ISBN: 978-1-4917-9901-7

Print information available on the last page.

iUniverse rev. date: 07/07/2016

Prologue

Shane Mac Lane invited Abbey and Kylie to stay in his mansion's carriage house while he worked on the *Copper Thieves* movie. Abbey looked at Filer. He took one look at the expression on Abbey's face and knew what his answer had to be.

Shane also offered Filer a chance to work as a stuntman/advisor on the picture because of the friendship they developed while Filer and his buddies built a distribution line between the main transmission line and Shane's isolated cabin in the Montana back country.

Abbey said, "We'll have to talk about it. Can I sleep on it?"

"Sure, talk it over and let me know."

After Shane left Filer said, "I don't know how much Shane is going to pay me. And how about your job, can you just walk away from it?"

"It sounds like you don't want me coming out to Hollywood with you."

That wasn't what Filer was thinking. What came to mind was that this was the first away from home job Abbey had shown any interest in during his career as a lineman.

"Of course I want you to come with me."

"I can take a leave of absence from my job. If things don't work out in California I'll come back and go back to work."

"We'll its settled then. We're all going to Hollywood.

"I'll call Shane in the morning," Abbey said with a smile.

Chapter 1

For the second time in his life Filer Wilson, a journey lineman looked off the top of a fifty foot pole into the rolling hills and meadows outside of Farewell Bend, Oregon. His climbing hooks were planted firmly in the pole and he leaned back comfortably into his leather safety belt. Memories from ten years earlier came back to him. He'd been an apprentice lineman then. Sure he was cocky and full of himself then. Those traits overrode any fear he'd had doing the dangerous work of stringing powerlines. Back then he'd made friends and enemies on his first job. Because the men around him had been boomers and not big company bureaucrats it was a little like the wild-west helping build his first power line.

This time around was very different from the first job.

"Okay you're fine right there," Bob Clifford, the second unit director called to Filer over a bull horn. Just stay right there."

Filer, the stuntman, came back to reality. "We'll shoot the scene where you and Chris Granger finished racing up the poles."

Filer recalled when Chris challenged him to the race because Chris thought he was too friendly with his wife Lou. Everyone had been surprised when the apprentice lineman blew the journey lineman away.

On a nearby pole another stuntman hung from his safety belt waiting for the director to do some more directing. He looked Filer's way and gave him a thumbs-up. Filer put a hand to his hard hat returning the respectful salute.

Filer looked back along the poles already in place. They crossed the gentle hilly land beside the Snake River. It was a pretty sight-one of the benefits of line work.

During the second phase of the job Filer and the rest of the crew would string high powered transmission lines. Until then the only danger on the pole was falling off of it. Falling could kill, or at least cripple him. His first experience of line work was watching a lineman burn a pole and die. That man's death had given him the chance to become an apprentice lineman. He was now a journey lineman-a position he was proud of.

He had other achievements he was proud of: Graduation from heavy equipment school and from Seabee training; and later with a field promotion to Second Class Petty Officer. When his tour with navy was finished he received an Honorable Discharge.

With his achievements came responsibilities; he had his mother Maggie, and Abbey and Kylie to take care of. He suspected they thought they were taking care of him. Hell, maybe they were right

All of these thoughts only took a minute. What happened next took Filer by surprise. The pole he was strapped to started growing. He felt it growing upward in slow motion. When he looked around he saw the nearby pole far below and he was dizzy from the height.

"Wait a minute, this must be a day dream, it can't be happening." This thought crossed his mind and he was back where he was supposed to be, at the top of a pole across from Chris' stuntman, waiting for the director.

The director huddled with his cameraman while he took shots of the two men at the top of the poles. When he was satisfied he brought the bull horn up and yelled, "Cut. Okay gentlemen, you can come down now."

Filer and the stuntman descended the poles and returned to the set seating area.

Two years earlier Filer took a job building steel towers in Montana. He was a journey lineman then going where the work took him. That's when his old ground man buddy Rupert Morby knocked on his trailer door and started asking for whatever Filer could remember about the

Farewell Bend job. He said he wanted his book *The Copper Thieves* to be as authentic as possible. Filer told him mostly he knew what he read in the papers back then and that the murderer Steve Williams had worked as a grunt on his crew.

"Whatever you can remember will be a big help," Rupert said. "Pretend we're drinking in a bar after work and telling tall tales for the rookies."

So, on his off hours away from home Filer 'Mad Dog' Wilson told Rupert what he remembered about the Farewell Bend job. Filer's recollections, plus a bunch of other 'tall tales' added by Rupert, turned into *The Copper Thieves*.

Rupert's first book would become a best seller, and then a movie.

"We're losing the light," the director said and then told the cast and crew to show up at Lou and Chris' store in the morning. "We'll be shooting back grounds for stringing wires, and the burglary scene."

On the way back to Ontario, Oregon where the cast and crew had rooms in a Holiday Inn Filer wondered what the first crew was shooting in the Hollywood studios. He assumed it didn't have much to do with climbing poles. A big part of *The Copper Thieves* had to do with the robbery and murder of Nicole Stickley, a local Idaho girl, who got hooked on drugs while trying to make the big time in San Francisco. She came back to Idaho as a drug dealer and got murdered for her efforts.

Filer was involved in the movie because the murderer, Steve Williams, had been on his crew.

After everyone got cleaned up at the Holiday Inn they all met up at the Wagon Wheel Bar. It hadn't changed much since Filer and the Rob Johnson boomers drank beers, chased barmaids and local women. Filer had met Abbey at the Wagon Wheel Bar.

Chapter 2

Steve Williams sat alone in a prison cell. He'd been in prison before, but this time he wasn't getting out. At times like this he relived the crime that landed him in prison with a life sentence. He'd only been out of the joint for six months when the urge to get his hands on easy money took over.

This urge was like an addiction. Williams couldn't overcome his addiction. He supposed it was like being an alcoholic. Part of the urge involved the adrenaline rush. In other words it was like needing a special kind of air to breath. Only a few people, special people who were in prison would know what he was talking about.

Really, he couldn't figure the big deal the authorities made out of his knocking off the drug dealing bitch. If the sheriff had caught the bitch dealing he would have had to arrest her and put her away. He'd saved society money by killing her."

Without much imagination Williams spent his time staring at the bare walls of his cell. He did have one thought on his mind. He would really like to even the score with the people who had put him in prison.

The more Williams thought about revenge the more it fueled his addiction. He needed the thoughts of hurting the people who put him behind bars to get through the long days. Later, thoughts didn't give him enough of the special air he needed to breathe. He had to up his game. He would make a list of the people who needed to follow Nicole. That would be the first step; the next would be finding a way to get to the people from inside his cell.

It wouldn't be impossible to get someone on the outside to maim and kill the people on his list.

At last Steve Williams had a purpose in his life to satisfy his needs.

Chapter 3

Kylie Wilson's life changed when she ended up in southern California with her mother and Filer. She knew Filer led a dangerous and exciting life as a lineman. Now because of Filer she was discovering a whole new kind of excitement. She had only vaguely followed celebrities back in Portland. Now it became a big thing living near Shane McLane at his Malibu mansion.

Of course she met the cast and crew of *The Copper Thieves*, and a lot of people just passing through the mansion.

Kylie and Abbey bought new clothes to fit the California climate, and the celebrities. Some of the clothes she bought didn't suit Filer. He would shake his head at short skirts and bikinis, but he didn't forbid her from wearing them. Kylie was twenty years old.

Shane also let Abbey and Kylie have the use of the low end of his stable of automobiles. This meant Jeeps and Japanese sedans were available to them. It was great. Kylie wasn't quite used to driving in L.A. traffic. It took a little nerve to get on the freeway and into downtown neighborhoods.

All of the kids her age who visited the mansion were Hollywood sophisticated. Kylie didn't like to admit that she envied them, and even less that she wanted to be like them.

Kylie gave up her boyfriend from Portland. Now she went to restaurants and clubs with Shane's younger friends.

Chapter 4

Jeffery Lodder started in Hollywood as a child star and was graduating into young adult rolls. Currently he acted in *American Daddy*, a modern *Father Knows Best* kind of sit-com where the father knows nothing and compensates by bullying everyone around him including his family.

Jeffery's moderate good looks with brown hair, amber eyes, and a gym built body earned him a place as the only son on *American Daddy*. At twenty-three years old Jeffery played the eighteen year old son.

Jeffery was spending his *American Daddy* money almost as fast as his parents had spent the money he earned doing earlier projects as a child star. Presently Jeffery's parents couldn't get within 1,000 feet of him because of a court order.

Along with spending his money Jeffery tried to seduce any female careless enough to get anywhere near him.

Kylie and Jeffery met in Shane's kitchen. It happened during an unusually quiet moment.

"Hey there," Jeffery greeted Kylie as she poured herself a glass of orange juice.

"Want some," Kylie asked, pointing the carton of orange juice at him?

"I was looking for a beer."

"In the fridge," Kylie replied, trying to stay calm. She recognized Jeffery from *American Daddy*. Kylie had watched a couple of episodes of *American Daddy* and decided family life as depicted on the show wasn't the way Filer treated Abbey or her.

"Have you been staying with Shane long," Jeffery asked?

"We're here while my dad works on *The Copper Thieves,*" Kylie said.

"Yeah, I heard about *Copper Thieves;* kind of a pet project for Shane."

Half an hour later Jeffery invited Kylie to go with him on the set of *American Daddy.* This was phase one of the Jeffery Lodder strategy. In Phase two Jeffery would tell Kylie that he would try to get her a chance for a walk on spot on the show.

Chapter 5

After the background footage for stringing the wires and for the burglary at Lou and Chris' store were filmed the second crew would return to Hollywood. The rest of the film would be filmed on a movie lot.

One week later Ted Johns, the union rep for the background filming unit, convinced the director to charter an old C47 to fly them back to Hollywood rather than taking the time to return via rail.

"You know time is money and going back by train will take three days. Flying back to L.A. we'll be back in an afternoon. The C47 has plenty of room for the crew and all of the gear. We'll unload everything ourselves and save time instead of waiting for porters to offload our stuff."

"Sometimes you do come up with a good idea," Clifford said. "Are you sure the plane can make the trip?"

"The pilot is a friend of mine. He's one of the best drug runners in the business."

Clifford gave Ted a startled look.

"Relax, Grant knows his business and he'll get us there no problem."

The crew loaded all of their cameras and film gear into the cargo hold of the C47, then climbed aboard and seated their selves in the passenger area. The pilot came into the passenger area and pointed to a toilet in the rear and said he hoped they had come with food because this flight was no frills.

"No problem," Ted said. "We're good," and he pointed to a cooler and basket with food in it.

Chapter 6

Ted sat next to Filer behind the director. The professional stuntman sat next to the director. Filer had struck up a friendship with Ted while they were drinking in the Wagon Wheel Bar. He'd learned that Ted was an operating engineer in the Army. This was the equivalent of being a Seabee in the Navy. Because theirs was a new friendship they hadn't heard all of each other's tall tales. Shortly after take-off Ted started a story about his service in the Nam.

"We were one hundred miles from the DMZ. A bunch of Green Berets had taken up residence in a French chateau in a small village by a strategic river crossing. The V.C. blew up the bridge and the Green Berets called up our platoon to come and rebuild the bridge.

When we arrived at the chateau, a Green Beret major put us up in a horse stable that was a part of the property.

Don't start feeling sorry for us. The horse stable hadn't stabled any horses for at least fifty years. When the Vietnamese chased the French out they took over the stable and converted it into living quarters. It wasn't the Ritz, but it was as good as, or better than a fire base out in the boonies.

So we got settled in and it took us about a month to rebuild the bridge. We hated to leave that little village by the chateau. It was like taking a vacation back to the fifties when the French were running the place and everything was nice and peaceful.

The Green Berets fixed up a shop in the village like a cabaret and they played French music on an old record player.

It was hard to tell whether the villagers liked having the Green Berets around, but they were giving away free medical care and they treated the villagers respectfully.

About a month after we got back to our permanent base in the rear I heard about a pretty French chateau and a little village that had been destroyed by the V.C. While they were blowing up our bridge they massacred the villagers and burned the surrounding farms. The Green Berets defended the village as long as they could and then they were evacuated by helicopters."

"Yeah, great story, what happened next?"

"Well, nothing next; a lot of healthy villagers died and the Green Berets went on to their next assignment."

"Sounds like the Nam. Hand me one of the beers."

"Sure. You want a sandwich? We've got tuna, ham and cheese, or bologna and cheese."

"Give me a beer and a tuna sandwich."

Chapter 7

Filer understood it was his turn to tell a tall tale.

"I was in-country at Rose Mary Point a year and a half when Chief Hansen called me and three other guys into a Quonset hut the officers and chiefs used as an office.

Chief Hansen stood us to attention and Lt. Parker came out of his office and stood by the chief.

I wondered what was going on. Maybe they had thought up some kind of extra duty. All I could do was stay at attention and wait for what was coming.

Lt. Parker said, "At ease Seabees. Take a seat."

I sat down with the rest of the men. There was a 1st class operator, one other 3rd class operator and a seaman 1st.

"Okay men, we've got a request here from a marine forward firebase."

The Lt. stopped, pausing for effect. "This assignment won't take more than three or four hours and you'll be back here safe and sound." The Lt. smiled at his little joke. "Chief, explain what the marines need."

"Yes sir." The chief stepped forward and sat on the edge of the table at the front of the room. "We're going to helo in some minis and build a helo pad for the fire base. This assignment will be called Operation Crane's Nest.

It's an easy assignment and you get to do a little sight- seeing."

Sonny raised his hand. He smiled, "I guess we volunteered for this assignment."

"Did you read anything that says the Seabees have to have your permission to give you any job it wants?"

15

"No chief," Sonny said taking the smile off his face.

"Alright then don't get your boxers in a twist. We got a company of marines there with an established perimeter. All they need is a raised hill leveled off into a helo pad. Like Lt. said we'll go up, stay a couple of hours and finish up in time for week-end liberty.

We'll be going to work in full battle gear."

Sonny spoke again, "When are we leaving chief?"

"We've got two Chinooks on the way here from Da Nang. We leave as soon as we get the minis hanging and ready to go. Right now we get our gear together and muster back here. We'll be going 1st class in a Huey." The chief had finished his explanation.

Lt. Parker dismissed the work party. "Chief Hansen this is your show. Keep me up to speed."

Lt. Parker went back to his office and Chief Hanson left to get his gear.

I walked to the barracks with the Charlie the seaman 1st class. Our base hadn't seemed like a safe place, but now it seemed a lot safer than a marine fire base out in the boonies.

"What the hell, I didn't come all the way here to hide out like a pussy."

I didn't know if this was exactly true but it helped get me in the mood to kick ass and take names.

Peter Thompson, the Peter, was the other 3rd class in the work detail. Charles Boyd, the seaman 1st, was a short-timer like me. We were both two months away from being sent back to the states to be honorably discharged.

As I saw it, it had been fun-like hell. I'd be happy to get on the next MAT flight back to the states and never think about Vietnam or the Seabees again. I wasn't a lifer like Chief Hansen or Sonny, the 1st class. When I got back to the states I'd get a construction job, chase women and drink beers after work with no problems.

"What about you Filer?" I tuned into Charlie's voice asking me a question.

"What?"

"Have you ever been to a firebase?"

"No, I've never been to a firebase."

"Do you think we'll be back in time for week end liberty?"

"I don't know anything more than you do. But it sounds like a simple dirt moving job."

Charlie said, "I don't know. Why did the Chief pick us?"

"Like the Chief said, 'Don't get your boxers in a twist. It's just another job. We get there with the minis, we knock down their hill and drink a few beers with the other boys in green and we're on our way back."

"If you say so man," Charlie said. Charlie looked up to Filer. Charlie knew how to operate a dozer, but apparently his father hadn't taught him how to man-up.

Clayton Wilson, Filer's dad, had included him in several extra-curricular adventures before Filer enlisted in the Seabees to avoid being drafted. Clayton was a leader. He was a railroad engineer and was responsible for freight and passengers whenever he took trains down the tracks. His charisma rubbed off on Filer.

After Charlie and I reported back to the Quonset hut with our battle gear Chief Hansen took us to the equipment yard and directed us to drive two of the mini dozers to the nearby airstrip so they could be harnessed up to the Chinooks when they arrived.

Chief Hansen sent Sonny and the other 3rd class ahead of the rest of us to the firebase. They were going to scout and clear a temporary landing zone for the minis. When they finished the temporary landing zone they would radio back they were ready to receive the minis.

An hour later we heard the chop, chop, chop air displacement of the first Chinook. The Chinook settled into the air space above the minis. The loading chief inside the Chinook contacted Chief Hansen and the two men coordinated harnessing the first mini to the Chinook's lifting and hauling gear.

Once we harnessed the minis on our end we would climb into the Huey and fly ahead of the minis to the firebase.

When we all got on the ground at the firebase we would get ready to receive the minis.

At the firebase Sonny met up with Gunny Rodriguez. The Gunny had already designated a temporary landing zone for the minis.

"Welcome to our firebase. We call her Foxtrot when she works; most of the time we call her firebase FUBAR.

Sonny and Thompson inspected the zone he picked and decided the Gunny had a good eye. Sonny radioed back to our base and gave us the go ahead.

Operation Crane's Nest was a go.

Chief Hansen directed our ground team harnessing up the minis.

With both the Chinooks loaded and circling overhead we jumped into the Huey and we were on our way to the firebase.

We arrived at the firebase and joined up with Sonny and the Peter at the temporary landing zone. The zone was just outside the firebase so Gunny Rodriguez had created a perimeter with his platoon. He made it clear we didn't have any time to lose getting the minis on the ground and inside the firebase. The Chinooks were right behind us and it only took us a half hour to get both of the minis unhooked and inside the firebase perimeter.

Everything was ready for leveling off the designated helo site. Sonny operated one of the minis and I operated the other mini.

The V.C. weren't stupid. We've had plenty of time to figure that out. As soon as they saw the Chinooks air lifting in the minis they figured something was up. So half way into Operation Crane's Nest all hell broke loose around the firebase. We were under mortar and ground attack. We stayed cool and continued pushing dirt off the hill top. Charlie and Thompson were guarding our six while the marines held the firebase's perimeter.

Filer paused for a minute to study Ted's expression. As he read it Ted was still interested.

"The V.C. was attacking," Ted prompted Filer.

"Yeah, you know what it sounds like in battle. You feel it in your muscles and drilling into your brain. It's hard to think of anything except how bad you want it to stop.

Well, we got the hill top leveled and drove the minis to the bottom of the hill.

The V.C. must have thought they scared us off because when the minis stopped pushing dirt they stopped attacking."

Ted smiled a little.

"The V.C. called off the attack, but not before they landed a mortar round dead center in the middle of the cleared off helo pad.

Filer again paused to see if Ted was following.

"Okay, so not a happy ending," Ted said.

Filer laughed, "No Seabees were injured or killed in Operation Crane's Nest."

"What about the crater in the middle of Crane's Nest?"

"The chief laughed when we asked him the same question."

"The chief explained, 'Those minis were never coming back to our base. You got to know the marines have operating engineers and it will be up to them to maintain the helo pad. Me and the Lt. wanted to give you guys some real combat experience. You don't know what it's like until you've been in it.'"

"I looked at Sonny and Charlie and could see they were thinking the same thing. "Holy shit we were just in it!"

The Huey settled onto the temporary landing zone the marines were protecting. We loaded into the chopper. The chief said, 'I want you men in the Lt.'s office after you stow your combat gear. We'll have a de-briefing.'"

"After we stowed our gear we mustered in the Lt.'s office. Chief Hansen was waiting for us and stood us to attention and told the Lt. we were ready for the de-briefing."

"Men, Chief Hansen has reported on Operation Crane's Nest. He tells me you preformed above and beyond during a V.C. attack on the Firebase. That's good to hear, so I'm offering each of you field promotions to your next ranks. Sonny that means you'll be a chief. Filer you and Thompson will be 2nd class petty officers and Charlie you'll be promoted from Seaman 1st to 3rd class. There is one stipulation you'll all have to agree to: you're all short-timers due to be discharged in the next 2 months or less. To accept your promotions you'll have to extend your enlistments for another year. Chief Hansen has the paper work you need to sign and take to the personnel office."

"The Lt. waited while the chief handed us our paper work. Sonny was a lifer so he signed first and handed his papers to the chief. Thompson and I signed up and handed Chief Hansen our papers. It took Charlie a little longer to decide what he was going to do until Chief Hansen explained there was also a signing bonus that went with the promotion. Charlie signed the papers and gave them to the chief.

Later the four of us ended up drinking beers at the enlisted men's club. Sonny came in with us until he could get chief's khakis. Charlie and I figured that's the last we'd see of him.

Chapter 8

Back on the C47 the two men drank their beers and ate their sandwiches. Then it was time to tilt back the seats and catch a nap. The next thing they heard was Grant telling them to fasten their seat belts and get ready for the landing.

"So, are you going to stay in La La Land and make more movies or go back to building power lines?"

"I've been giving it some thought and I think I'll go back to equipment operating. The work isn't as seasonal as line work, and I can stay closer to my family."

"Have you reached out, sent out any resumes yet?"

"No resumes. I still have to decide where I want to work."

"How about going to Vegas with me and the crew? You can use the down time to ponder your next move?"

Ted's invitation made sense to Filer. Except for the jobs he was assigned to out of the IBEW-International Brotherhood of Electrical Workers union hall he'd always got on to jobs through people he knew and otherwise through word of mouth. Someone said someone was hiring and you should check it out.

"I haven't totally made up my mind and I have to talk to Abbey before I do."

For the next ten minutes Filer and Ted finished their beers in silence.

Once the vintage cargo flier was on the ground and the movie gear was unloaded into a company van, the crew dropped Filer off at Shane's place.

Chapter 9

Shane McLane's Malibu mansion held Shane's extended family and all of his entourage comfortably. When he first arrived at Shane's place Filer asked himself why one man needed a mansion for himself. Over the months he watched people come and go like the mansion was a hotel. He saw producers, directors; other actors and the occasional long lost cousin come and go. He began to understand that Shane did indeed have a good reason for having a mansion.

The house staff acted more like guests who performed occasional duties rather than menial servants. Despite this or maybe because of this the household ran very smoothly. Meals were served at set times and guests who weren't present for these meals were welcome to prepare their own mini meals.

Except for rare incidents guests respected Shane's attitude towards the staff and those who didn't were invited to find quarters elsewhere.

Filer entered the carriage house and expected to see Abbey and Kylie. He saw Abbey reading a script. It seemed to Filer that everyone in Hollywood was obsessed with the movie business. He guessed that's why it was called dream land. People either wanted to write, direct, produce, or act in some kind of fantasy about real life. He hadn't written the *Copper Thieves*, he'd done better, he'd lived it. Rupert, his one-time ground man had written the book that Shane McLane was turning into an action movie.

Abbey put the script aside and asked Filer if wanted to eat dinner. "I could eat."

After preparing dinner Abbey and Kylie sat down with Filer.

"This is good," Filer complimented Abbey.

"As good as restaurant food?"

"You know how I feel about restaurant food."

"They have a lot of good restaurants here."

"It's not about the restaurants. It's about being with family."

Abbey put down her knife and fork and sat quietly for a minute.

"I guess that's a compliment."

Filer looked at Abbey and smiled his Mad Dog smile.

Once Filer and Abbey had finished eating they cleared the dishes and went into the living room to watch TV together. Abbey was quiet for a while and then she said, "Kylie met an actor and he's getting her a walk on part on *American Daddy*." Abbey stopped again and waited to make sure she had Filer's attention.

"Kylie's an adult, at least according to the law. She can do what she wants."

"Sure, but he invited us to come see her walk on part."

Filer gave her a raised eyebrow. "Well, you know what Hollywood is like."

Abbey smiled and said, "A bunch of scumbags."

Filer smiled back. He glanced away from the TV and asked, "What do you want to do?"

"This scumbag invited us to watch Kylie on the set of *American Daddy*."

"We're both adults," Filer said, "We know what he really wants."

"He may not be that bad, at least he wants to get to know us."

"What did you tell Kylie?"

"I told her I'd ask you if you'd come with us."

"I'll do it," Filer said.

The next morning Filer had a meeting with Shane in the post-production offices of *Copper Thieves*.

Chapter 10

Shane greeted Filer in his office, "Hey Filer."

Filer nodded at Shane and sat down in a chair facing Shane's desk.

"You know as producer of *Copper Thieves* I have to put together the different elements of what we've shot and come up with the finished product."

"That's Hollywood stuff that you get the big bucks for."

"What big bucks? As the producer I'm putting up my own money for a pet project. But, as you know I believe in this project because I was there. I know it's real, anyway close to real."

Filer smiled. "It's all lies except for the true parts."

"Yeah I guess truth is stranger than fiction. But you have to admit we had a hell've of a good time rescuing Rip-It-Up. Do you remember Cherie with her big pistol?"

"It was a real party," Filer said.

"Okay, the movie is done except for the finishing touches." Shane paused and looked a little uncomfortable. "You and Abbey and Kylie are welcome to stay in the carriage house as long as you want."

"I get it. You're kicking us out."

"No, I'm just saying you'll probably want to get back to work now that your job as an advisor/stuntman on the movie is done."

"You don't think I can make it as a stunt man?" Filer smiled.

When we make another movie where we need a lineman I'll give you a call. But really most of the stuntmen we hire have gone to stuntman school or they've been doing it so long we can't get rid of them."

Even if it wasn't true Filer said he was working on a couple leads for work.

Chapter 11

Abbey and Kylie were out doing what they loved-shopping for more clothes than they needed, so Filer had the rest of the day for himself. He met up with Ted at a Mexican place for Tequila shots and tacos.

"I'm taking the crew to Vegas," Ted explained. "We'll be staying overnight at a casino. Maybe we'll take in a show; get drunk afterwards; raise a little hell, lose some chips; and get back to L.A. in time to go to work on our next picture on Monday morning."

"Want to go along?"

"What do I tell Abbey?"

"'There is that," Ted replied, and then smiled. "Tell her she's welcome to come along and take in a show. If she says yes you're set. She'll probably take a pass when you tell her you're going with me and the crew, and let you go anyway."

"I'll think about it," Filer said.

"You can tell her it's a tradition for our crew when we finish a movie. If she's into the Hollywood thing that'll make it okay."

Chapter 12

Later, Filer drove back to Malibu and walked into the empty carriage house. He cleaned up and started watching a little TV. About an hour later Abbey and Kylie got home. He didn't ask where they had been. They had shopping bags enough that told the story. Just after Abbey got ready for bed and was getting comfortable beside Filer he used Ted's plan. He was surprised when Abbey chose option A. He could go to Vegas with the boys. Abbey didn't want to leave Kylie alone. The next day Filer drove into the L.A. to Ted's place.

"Well, how did it go," Ted asked?

Filer looked a little disappointed and waited for a reaction from Ted. Ted also looked disappointed. "Well anyway you tried, huh."

"What do you mean, Best Boy? I got a green light for plan A."

"Great," Ted patted Filer on the shoulder.

Chapter 13

Back at the mansion Filer came into the living room and saw Kylie sitting on the sofa with a slick Hollywood type. He had an arm draped over her shoulder. He reminded Filer of a couple of her boyfriends back in Portland. This one already had a smirk on his face. Filer walked into the room and he remained sitting beside Kylie.

"Hi dad," Kylie greeted Filer.

"What's up?" Filer said.

"I'm going to do a walk-on on *American Daddy* with Jeffery. It's a TV show and he's one of the stars. He thinks he might get me a real part if the director likes me." Kylie continued explaining. "I'll be the 'wanna' be girl friend of the son of the family."

Filer didn't say anything and went into the kitchen to get a glass of water.

Jeffery looked at Kylie silently asking the question, "What the hell?"

"Well dad, what do you think?"

"I haven't seen the show so I don't think anything."

Filer sat back in his recliner and Girlfriend jumped into his lap. Filer glimpsed another smirk on Jeffery's face. He was starting to take a real dislike to this young punk.

"Mr. Wilson, how about visiting the set and you can see what *American Daddy* is all about. Give us a chance to show you Kylie will be treated like any other actor on the show."

"I'm going to Vegas this weekend so whatever you're doing will have to wait until next week."

"Okay, I can work with that. I promise you Kylie will love being on the show."

Filer patted Girlfriend.

Chapter 14

The next morning when Filer woke up Abbey was already up. He showered, packed an overnight bag and went to the kitchen to see about breakfast.

Abbey greeted him, "Good morning sweetie. What do you want for breakfast?"

"Eggs, bacon and toast are always good."

Abbey asked Filer how much money he would need for his trip between coffee and eggs and bacon.

Filer smiled, "How much can you give me?"

Abbey smiled back at him and didn't say anything.

"I'll probably have to buy a couple of rounds of drinks. Ted mentioned we would be taking in a show. I think two or three hundred dollars will be okay, and if I don't need it I'll bring back what's left over."

Abbey went into the bedroom and came back with a small roll of bills. "Behave yourself while you're there."

Filer smiled, "You know I always behave myself when I'm away from home."

Chapter 15

Filer took a look at Ted's Bronco when he stopped in the carriage house driveway. "All you need is a canvas water bag hanging off the mirror."

"Sorry old buddy, I guess we'll just have to make do with a cooler full of ice and beers. We did throw in a couple of gallons of water in case the radiator overheats."

Filer nodded his head and got into the passenger seat.

"We're going to pick up two other guys from the crew. We've been working pretty hard and we need a little break."

Ted made his way through downtown L.A. into the suburbs and stopped at a small Spanish style ranch house with a chain link fence surrounding it. He honked the horn and a large man in a muscle T-shirt exited the house. He climbed into a rear seat of the Bronco.

Filer knew all of the crew and nodded at George Rogers. Everyone called him Mr. Rogers. It never got old.

"Get yourself a beer," Ted said.

"Okay, it's a little early but this is a road trip."

After one more stop Ted had assembled his crew. They all had beers and the road trip was off to a good start.

A road sign advertised a Coming Attraction at a last gas for 75 miles station. The station also had a souvenir shop.

Ted asked, "What do you guys think?"

"I've got to pee," John Farr laughed. "It's your fault, you gave us the beers."

"Okay, I guess we could all use a break."

Filer smiled and remembered all of the road trips he had taken with his family traveling between Portland, Oregon and Riverview, Idaho. Someone always had to pee in the middle of the trip.

This trip was different because the landscape they were traveling was a dry desert. Filer thought it might be a good idea to stop and check the engine. He didn't want to end up stranded in the middle of the desert and he also had to pee.

Ted pulled the Bronco into a dirt parking lot and stopped by the single gas pump. He got out of the Bronco and started pumping gas. The passengers got out and headed for the men's rest room. It was only big enough for one man so they took turns using the toilet. By the time they were all through Ted had filled the truck up, topped off the radiator and checked the oil. Everything looked okay.

Ted took his turn in the restroom and then joined everyone in the souvenir shop. He paid for the gas and went to where his crew was observing the small zoo maintained by the station proprietor.

"I'll bet you guys haven't ever seen a half donkey, half zebra before."

Mr. Rogers said, "You're right John. This is the first time I've seen a Zedonk, very interesting."

The men walked by cages that held a rattlesnake, a Gela monster, and an owl.

After a last stop in the souvenir shop to buy ice for the ice chest Ted led the crew back to the Bronco; and they were on their way across the desert.

"Next stop Vegas," Ted said.

The desert went by at 80 miles an hour, and soon the men spotted a green valley in the desert.

"We're here boys," Ted said. "Let's find a place to stay so we can go out and start gambling."

Chapter 16

The crew checked into the Sunrise Motel two men to a room. Filer roomed with Ted. It wasn't the first time he'd bunked with another man. He'd spent plenty of time in barracks in the Seabees. Both men got their gear out of the Bronco and stowed it in the motel room. Twenty minutes later they were ready to party.

It was four o'clock and they decided to have a look around before they settled into a casino for some serious gambling. Ted drove the Bronco along the strip watching the marque signs. They passed Caesar's Palace and Harrah's Club. Then they settled on MGM Grand for their first stop.

Inside the casino Ted and Filer stopped at the dollar slots. The rest of the crew split up between the 21 table and the craps table.

Filer and Ted played the slots for an hour and barely got their money back. Filer suggested, "You know when you've been playing a slot for a while and finally get up and a little old lady with grey hair sits down and hits the jack-pot."

"Yeah, I know what you mean," Ted answered.

"Let's change slots and see what happens."

"Okay, you're on. Let's do it."

Ted and Filer got up and changed machines. They played for another five minutes until Ted hit the jack-pot.

"That would never happen again," Ted said. "Anyway we'll split this pot. Let's keep playing and see if you hit."

They played for another ten minutes and Filer said, "I think we've played our luck out on these slots. Let's see what the rest of the crew is doing."

They found George playing 21. He looked unhappy.

"How are you doing George?" Ted asked.

"I'm down a hundred. I guess I'm ready to get out of here."

"Good man. Let's go find John."

George grabbed the chips he had left and walked away from the 21 table with Ted and Filer.

The trio of men looked across the casino and spotted John at the craps table.

John threw the dice and rolled a five. The croupier retrieved the dice and passed them to John. John blew on the dice and rolled them while the rest of the crew watched. The dice danced across the green felt and tipped into snake eyes.

"Next shooter," the croupier called out.

With the crew together Ted led them out of the casino into the warm night air.

"Okay, time for dinner. Let's find an all you can eat place and think about taking in a show."

The men finished a big meal washed down with coffee. Ted collected money for the check and tipped the waitress.

On the way back to their motel Filer looked out his window and did a double take. "Stop here," Filer said.

Chapter 17

"What's up?" Ted wanted to know.

"Go back to the club on my side of the street. I saw a band I know up on a sign."

Ted turned the Bronco around and drove them back to a place called the Blue Lagoon. On their marque the sign read: Rip-It-Up Roberts and the Rippers.

"Who's Rip-It-Up Roberts?" Ted wanted to know.

"Rip-It-Up and I go back a ways. He was playing at the Wagon Wheel Bar and Restaurant when I worked in Farewell Bend, Oregon.

The group of men followed Filer into the Blue Lagoon Lounge where a crowd sat listening to Rip-It-Up Roberts and the Rippers playing their way through an oldie but a goodie. They took a seat in the half empty lounge near the stage. At the end of the song Filer clapped loudly and Rip-It-Up saw him.

"Folks we're going to take a break. Don't go anywhere and we'll be right back."

Rip-It-Up jumped down from the stage and walked towards Filer with a big grin on his face.

"Hey Filer, your old buddy Ozzie told me you're a Hollywood star now." Rip-It-Up turned a chair around backwards and sat down at their table.

"No, I'm just a small part of the movie. I'm an advisor/stuntman."

Rip-It-Up laughed and said. "How about getting me a part in the Montana kidnapping and showdown. I think I know pretty much all that happened."

"Sorry that's gotta wait for the sequel. But I'll remind Rupert you were there."

Rip-It-Up laughed and stood up. "Okay Mad Dog I'll be looking forward to the sequel." Rip-It-Up went back to the stage.

Filer had slipped back into Mad Dog mode while Rip-It-Up was at the table and it brought a slight smile to his lips. Line work had been good to him. The time he'd spent away from line work so far seemed like a strained vacation. He knew he had to go back to it. The men around him were laughing and talking. He sat silently with his thoughts of going back to work away from Hollywood. It didn't take much thinking to know Abbey and Kylie had taken to the Hollywood lifestyle more than he had. What would their reaction be to going back to the old lifestyle now that they knew how the rich and famous lived?

When he first met Abbey he was chasing work and women. After their wedding he had a family and only had to chase work. Now, in Hollywood he felt like he was chasing family again.

Chapter 18

"Hey Filer, what's on your mind old buddy?"

Filer broke out of his reverie when he heard Ted's question.

"Well, I guess I'm thinking about what's going to happen now that the picture is finished. I know I'll have to go back to work and it's getting harder to stay in the northwest. If I want to work I'll have to move around more and be away from my family."

"Why don't you stay in Hollywood?"

"Hollywood's not my thing. It's okay working with you guys, but the rest of it is a little above my pay grade. All the stuff with directors and stars is a little hard to take."

Ted said, "I had the same problem when I first started out. You just have to ignore the bullshit and take those people as people if they say or do something you don't like. Treat them like you'd treat a man on one of your crews. I'll admit it doesn't always work with the really self-centered assholes, but most of them will respect you for it."

"That sounds sensible," Filer replied.

"If you do decide you don't want to stay in Hollywood I might be able to find you some kind of work. You have construction and heavy equipment experience with the Seabees."

"Yeah, I learned a little bit in Vietnam," Filer said.

"The strong silent type like in the movies," Ted laughed.

"Yeah, that's me, the strong silent type."

"Let me know when you're getting ready to leave tinsel town and I'll talk to some people."

Filer nodded and then paid attention while Rip-It-Up sang his version of *Lay, Lady, Lay*. He did surprisingly well.

Later, back at the Sunrise Motel he laid awake trying to make up his mind about whether to stay in Hollywood, go back to Portland, or to try for a job even further from home. With heavy equipment work he could stay in a place longer. He'd make good money. It wouldn't be as exciting as line work, whatever that meant. Probably it meant he couldn't get electrocuted or fall to his death from one hundred feet in the air. As he laid thinking of his future he listened to Ted snoring and thought of staying in the Seabees barracks in Vietnam. Little by little he fell asleep.

Chapter 19

After another day spent gambling, Filer had stayed even. He paid for his meals and a couple of rounds of drinks for the movie crew and was ready to go home, even though that only meant going back to Shane's guest house.

On the way back to California there was a lot of talk about who won and who lost. Filer stayed quiet. He knew the movie was finished except for post-production. Now he had to make a decision concerning the next part of his life. Maybe he wouldn't be making the same decision for Abbey and Kylie.

Chapter 20

At the carriage house Filer unloaded his travel bag and gave Ted's crew a good-bye salute. It was late afternoon and Abbey and Kylie were waiting inside the carriage house.

"Hi dad," Kylie greeted Filer.

"What's up?" Filer replied.

"You promised to watch my walk on roll on *American Daddy*."

"I remember. When is it happening?"

"Jeffery is still talking to the director."

Later during dinner Abbey asked, "What are you thinking Filer?"

"I've made up my mind to try to find work as an equipment operator."

"That sounds good to me," Abbey said and then asked, "What about P.G. & E.? Can you go back to Portland?"

"You know how seasonal that work is if I went back to line work; I want to get a steady equipment operating job."

Abbey said, "I guess we'll just have to make those decisions as they come up."

Chapter 21

The next day Filer heard the doorbell ring. He was alone in Shane's carriage house while Abbey and Kylie were out star gazing. That's what he called it anyway. He walked to the door and opened it. Shane smiled at him from the door step.

"Hey Mad Dog, have you got a minute?"

"Sure. Come in," Filer said and smiled back at his friend. He didn't need to go out star gazing. Here was a star standing in front of him.

"Want a beer?" Filer asked when they got to the living room off of the kitchen.

"Yeah, I could drink a beer."

Filer pulled two long necked beers from the fridge and sat down with Shane.

"I just got word that *Copper Thieves* is done except for a little post-production," Shane said. He looked at Filer to see if he guessed why he was sitting and drinking a beer with him.

Filer got the hint. "I guess I'm out of a job."

"Well the movie is out of our hands now. The next time we see it will be at the opening, red carpet and all."

"Abbey and Kylie will want to be here for that."

"What about you?"

"You know I've got to go back to making a living."

Shane smiled, "That's kind of why I'm here. My manager thinks he can get you a commercial. It might pay enough so Abbey and Kylie could stay here for the premiere."

"Man, I don't know. I'm not an actor."

"Are you kidding me? You've got a great sense of timing when you've got something to say. And anyway the commercial's director takes care of the script and the action. All you have to do is smile and raise an eyebrow. I've seen you do that dozens of times. So what do you say Mad Dog?

You already have a Sag card because of your work as a stunt man on *Copper Thieves*. All you have to do is show up at the studio for the audition. All I have to do is give Chet the word and he'll sit it up for you."

Filer sat silently for a minute sipping his beer, and then he smiled and raised an eyebrow.

"Good man," Shane said. "Chet will get in touch with the details. Remember whatever happens this is La La Land and everyone in the business knows it. Don't take any of it too seriously. That's the secret. They can't hassle you if you know the secret."

Shane stood up to leave and he put out his hand to shake hands with Filer. Filer walked him to the door. Shane left the carriage house and Filer went back to the fridge to get another beer.

Later when Abbey and Kylie came back Filer debated if he should tell them about the commercial. While they ate dinner Filer listened to the two women in his life talk about the stars they only thought they had seen. As he listened he thought it would be a cool surprise if the first thing they knew of the commercial would be seeing it on TV so he decided not to tell them before the commercial was made.

For the rest of the evening Filer listened to Abbey and Kylie. It was a little different from him being the story teller talking about his day.

Life in Hollywood had changed the relationships in his family. Now Abbey had something more interesting going on than her work at the Grocery Superstore; and Kylie was getting into the Hollywood scene. She had signed up to be an extra on *Copper Thieves* and now she wanted more work as an extra. Once she was on the set of a movie as an extra she could star gaze to her heart's content.

"Okay, maybe doing a commercial would give me something to talk about," Filer thought.

After dinner and a little TV Filer and Abbey went to bed. Filer was surprised to be in the mood for sex but Abbey wasn't. That was that.

Chapter 22

The next morning Filer ate breakfast with Abbey and Kylie and then they were out the door. Abbey was going with Kylie to get some 8x10 headshots for her audition portfolio. The 8x10's weren't necessary because extras just answered a call and showed up in crowds for the casting director to pick and choose. Getting the 8x10's was a way of being a part of the scene for Abbey and Kylie.

Shortly it was just Filer and Girlfriend in the carriage house. He was waiting for Chet, Shane's manager, to call with the information he needed to audition for the commercial. According to Shane the commercial would be an easy paycheck.

Girlfriend purred contentedly as Filer petted her. At ten o'clock the phone rang. Chet asked Filer if was interested in doing the commercial.

"I'm in," Filer said.

"Okay," Chet said and gave Filer an address to go to for the audition. "Don't worry about the audition. It's a formality only. Stop at a Woolworths and get one of their photo machine photo strips to leave with the casting director."

"Don't I need 8x10's?"

"Not necessary. Just get them the photo strip with a couple of different expressions on the strip so they remember you after the audition."

"What is the commercial advertising?"

"Does it matter?"

"I guess not," Filer admitted, "as long as they pay."

Chapter 23

Filer stopped at a strip mall with a mini Woolworths. It had been a long time since he'd spent nickels and dimes in a five and ten cent store. Now-a-days a good Woolworths sold everything Montgomery Wards sold; maybe at a cheaper price and quality, but basically the same merchandise.

Just inside the double doors Filer found the photo booth. He stepped inside the booth and put his money in the slot. When the go light went on he made faces at the lens. He smiled, frowned, raised an eyebrow and gave the lens a sideways profile. "That's enough," he said. He couldn't help smiling and made a quick circuit of the store reliving childhood memories. After the trip down memory lane Filer stepped out the glass double doors into the bright blue California sky, "Time to get on the yellow brick road."

Following Chet's directions Filer drove to a small store front building in another strip mall. It didn't look like a studio. Filer double checked the address he'd written down and he was where he was supposed to be.

The store front window signage advertised Excel Promotions. Filer read his note and knew he was in the right place. He took a deep breath and opened the tinted doors.

Inside the store front a receptionist ruled the waiting area. Filer walked to her desk.

"Name?" the petite blonde asked.

"Filer Wilson."

"Would that be Mad Dog Wilson?"

"Yeah that's my work nickname."

"Mr. Beckford has you down for a two o'clock appointment." She looked at the lobby clock and pointed at a chair opposite her desk.

Filer sat down to wait the fifteen minutes until his appointment.

Filer looked at the decorations on the reception walls and recognized some of the commercial posters. It looked like the place was legit. The fifteen minutes passed quickly and then the receptionist said, "Mr. Wilson Mr. Beckford will see you now," then she pointed at a door to go through.

"Here we go," Filer said to himself.

The inside of the room was larger than Filer thought it would be. As far as he could compare it to a movie set it looked to have all the equipment for making a commercial. The far end of the room had a raised platform for a stage. A director's chair and cameras occupied the center of the room. All of the extras he'd seen before, lighting, reflectors, and sound booms on extender poles were there.

A man of medium height entered the room from a door with a unisex toilet sign above it.

"Hi, Mr. Wilson, or do you want to be called Mad Dog?"

"Mad Dog is okay. It's my work name."

"Well my name is Earnest Beckford. You can call me Earnie."

The two men shook hands.

"So you want to make a commercial?"

"I thought you were the one who wanted to make a commercial," Filer said and smiled.

"Good one," Earnie said.

"Seriously, my friend Shane McLane and his manager set this up for me."

"Let's see your head shots."

"Yeah here they are," Filer said and handed him the strip of Woolworth photos.

Filer was curious, "You don't need 8x10's?"

"Actually Chet and Shane told me you'd do this and I respect their judgment. This is just for my files. I've got to have them for insurance purposes."

"I understand," Filer said.

"Problem is the person we're doing the commercial for isn't here yet. She's late.

Listen when Dyna Rees gets here don't be fooled by her looks. She runs a top Hollywood martial arts dojo for women. I run the lights and camera but Dyna does the fight scene choreography. I'm sure if you do exactly what she says you won't get hurt."

"What the hell. I'm getting into it with a female Bruce Lee," Filer thought.

Earnie showed Filer his camera, range finder and light meter. He seemed a little nervous to Filer.

The door to the studio opened and a Hispanic man with a buzz cut came into the room.

"Sorry boss, lunch ran a little long."

"No problem. She's not here yet.

Filer this is Juan. He's my assistant."

Filer nodded at Juan.

The door opened again and a well-muscled red head entered the room. She walked confidently to stand in front of Earnie.

"You ready to get this done?"

"If you're ready we're ready."

Dyna looked at Filer sizing him up as an opponent.

"Do you know why you're here man?"

"His name is Filer," Earnie said.

"It's Mad Dog," Filer corrected Earnie and looked at Dyna.

"I run a martial arts program for ladies. It's mainly a self-defense program showing ladies how they can protect themselves. I build confidence in them by giving them basic self-defense skills."

Dyna looked at Filer to see if he was paying attention.

"I have a wife and daughter so I can appreciate what you're doing."

Dyna kept giving Filer a hard stare trying to see if he was the kind of man who enjoyed smacking women around.

"You don't need to look at me like that. Abbey and I are partners."

"Okay then, I'm going to show you some moves I want you to make against me.

Earnie we need a couple of minutes to go through some moves and then you can start filming."

Earnie said, "How about if I film a little action for additional just-in-case footage?"

"Sounds good," Dyna said.

Dyna led Filer to the stage where a padded exercise mat covered most of the platform.

"We're going to do some practice moves Mad Dog," Dyna said with a slight smile.

Filer didn't smile and he didn't frown. He looked at Dyna and said, "I was in the Seabees and as part of our training we had marine combat training. I'm going to follow your lead and I don't want to hurt you so you should tell me what you want before we get into this."

"I appreciate that Mad Dog. Thanks for the heads-up. I've been doing this for ten years and I have Black Belts in Ju-Jitsu and Karate. I didn't open Dynamo Dojo for Women because I saw a couple of Kung Fu movies."

Filer nodded.

"We'll go through everything in slow motion first. No surprises."

Filer smiled. He was starting to feel more comfortable.

"The first demonstration is to counter a front grab." Dyna posed Filer as an assailant trying to grab a woman from the front.

What I'm going to do is counter this move by bringing my arms up inside your forearms and breaking your hold. Then I'm going to stomp my foot down on the inside of your ankle and then jab my hand into your throat. I promise I won't do any of these moves hard enough to cause any permanent damage."

Earnie and Juan were busy filming just-in-case footage.

Dyna put Filer back into the starting position for an assailant. She and Filer went through the moves she had laid out until the movements were coming smoothly.

For the next hour Earnie filmed Filer and Dyna going through the choreographed attack and defend movements.

Finally Dyna left the exercise mat and spoke to Earnie. "I think we've got enough to do what we need to make the commercial. We can do my stand-up and a voice over to finish it up."

"You took the words out of my mouth," Earnie said.

Dyna went back to the exercise mat and explained what was next.

"We've got what we need for the commercial. Now you just wait for your check from your agency.

You know Filer you've got something and I could probably pay you money to work out with the girls at the Dojo. They'd get a thrill out of pushing a big guy like you around," Dyna said and handed Filer her card.

Earnie walked to Dyna and then said to Filer, "Dyna's right. You're a natural. The camera loves you. I might have more work for you in the future. I'll send today's paper work to your agency."

"When will the commercial be on TV," Filer asked?

"It'll be ready next week," Earnie said.

Filer watched Dyna leave the studio. It was in his thoughts that he hadn't felt the way he was affected by Dyna since he married Abbey. He hadn't been physically close to another woman in all the years of his marriage. Here next to him in the studio Dyna was an attractive physically fit woman. Her business card had the same smell of perfume he'd sensed when they were close together on the exercise mat.

Chapter 24

On Kylie's first day on the set of *American Daddy* the Wilson family left Shane's guest house together. They arrived at the *American Daddy* set a little early.

The set was dark as they sat in audience seats waiting for the actors and production crew to appear. Minutes after they sat down a young woman with a clip board appeared.

"You must be Kylie. No one explained how this all works, huh?"

"Uh no," Kylie said.

"Well, all the actors are in make-up. They've been here since five-thirty. Come with me."

"What about my parents?"

"They'll have to wait here. Or they can go to the studio cafeteria and have breakfast."

The assistant gave Filer and Abbey back stage passes that gave them access to the cafeteria.

"I guess I'll see you later," Kylie said.

"Good luck sweetie," Abbey said. Then she smile and said, "I guess I should have said, Break a leg."

The assistant smiled and led Kylie away.

Filer had experience with being on a movie set, but no experience on a TV set. Now he'd see if there was any difference between the two.

"Let's go get a cup of coffee," he told Abbey. After sitting over a long cup of coffee Filer and Abbey returned to the set and showed a guard their back stage passes. They took seats with several other audience members.

A red light came on that read, "Quiet on set."

The lead actors were on the set ready for the director to call action.

Filer noticed the father and son were dressed normally for a trip outside the house, or a casual day at home, but the mother and daughter looked like they might be got up as streetwalkers.

The director called action and Filer heard language from all the family members he'd only heard working around laborers his whole working career. He started to wonder what his adopted daughter was getting herself into, even if it was just a one-time walk on role.

Fifteen minutes into the episode after a couple of starts and stops it was time for Kylie's walk on as the son's latest girlfriend.

Kylie came on stage in a getup just a little less hooker-like than the other two women. She had a single line. She said, "Hi," to the son. Her part put her sitting down between the father and son, and both of them put hands on her knees.

"Cut, cut, cut," the director said. "Kylie, don't frown and look scared. Smile and look friendly."

"Alright, let's do another take."

This time through Kylie looked less stressed and put on a smile.

"That's better," the director said and then said, "Okay let's do it again."

Filer sensed Abbey was a little uncomfortable with this scene. But the behavior on the set got the audience going. Whenever the audience wrangler held up the applause sign they clapped and hooted and hollered. The wrangler gave a hands lowered signaling to bring the applause down. The crowd caught on and made less noise right on cue.

Filer had seen enough and when Kylie left the set he asked Abbey if she wanted to leave. From his movie experience he knew there was a long day still ahead on the *American Daddy* set.

"No, I'm going to stay until Kylie's done. We can catch a taxi home."

In parting Filer said, "I'm not impressed with the show so far. I think the show treats women badly."

"It's just a TV show, Filer. That's not what those people are like in real life."

"I'm not sure that's true," Filer said. "Sometimes these actors play to their type. You know they are who they are."

"We'll see you at home sweetie," Abbey said.

At the carriage house after giving Kylie's situation some thought Filer took out Dyna's card and called her.

Chapter 25

After calling Dyna Filer met up with Ted at a local bar.

"What's up my man?"

"I'm enjoying my time between jobs. What's up with you, Mad Dog?"

"Abbey and I went to see Kylie in her walk on role with *American Daddy*." Filer raised an eyebrow when he finished his sentence.

"Looks like you weren't impressed."

"Not my taste. If I want to see porn I can always order it at a motel while I'm on the job; if I looked at porn, which I don't."

"You know some shows have a reputation. *American Daddy* has a bad rep. People say the director treats his talent badly, and the actors pick up on that and their behavior off the set isn't much better than on the set."

"Kylie met the son on the sit-com at Shane's place and he got her a walk-on spot. Maybe this whole thing will be over when they finish this episode. Anyway Abbey will be with her until she finishes her walk-on."

Ted changed the subject, "Have you given any thoughts to staying here now that *Copper Thieves* is finished?"

"I thought about it, but I don't think I'll be staying. This town isn't my kind of place. I guess it's okay if you know what you're doing, but I don't have that kind of experience."

"You don't have to worry about hurting my feelings. I was in your shoes about ten years ago and I still wonder if I made the right decision staying out here. This place makes construction site politicking look like grade school stuff."

"Anyway, if you think you're going back to the real world let me have a resume and I'll check around and see what's happening; might get lucky."

Filer sipped his beer and nodded his head. After all that's the way he'd gotten most of his jobs, through word of mouth and friends. It didn't hurt to be signed up at the union hall either.

Chapter 26

A week later, after Abbey had photocopied an updated resume for Filer and he'd given it to Ted. Ted called him back.

"Hey old buddy I've got some good news. I got a call back on your resume from a friend in the construction business in Nevada. What do you think about being a gold miner?"

Filer didn't answer. Then Ted said, "Filer, you still there?"

"Yeah, I'm here."

"Well, what do you think?"

"I don't know anything about mining gold."

"You don't have to know anything about gold. All you have to know is how to operate heavy equipment and maybe how to drive a truck."

"I can do that."

"Okay. The job interview is in Winnemucca, Nevada on Friday. See me at the club and I'll give you all the details."

"When would the job start?"

"Don't know exactly, but I think sooner rather than later."

Filer hesitated for a minute then he said "Thanks Ted. I'll call you as soon as I talk it over with Abbey."

Chapter 27

When Kylie came home after her guest appearance on *American Daddy* she was anxious to hear Filer's opinion on the show. She thought she hadn't been treated very well, but on the show she was just a character. Whatever had happened to her character hadn't happened to her, it had happened to her character. She was afraid Filer wouldn't understand that. She walked into the kitchen and saw Filer and her mom sitting at the kitchen table which was really a marble island.

"Hi dad," she didn't ask what he thought. "Guess what? The director said the audience really liked me."

Filer looked at Abbey and then said, "Kylie, the audience liked how the father and son on the show disrespected you. I'm surprised at you. Your mother would leave me if I treated either one of you like that."

With a quick glance at Abbey Kylie said, "Dad, you know what happened was just a show."

"If it was just a show then it's a bad show," Filer said.

"I might get a part on the show. Jeffery said he'll get his agent to represent me."

Filer toned down his expression from a raised eyebrow to a silent stare.

"Will the agent have any say in how your character is treated on the show?"

"I don't know about that," Kylie replied. "But I want to be on the show."

Filer looked at Abbey, "What do you think?"

"It's just a show. They're acting. Jeffery seems like a nice kid when he's here."

"I don't like to see you dressing the way you do on the show; and even if it's only acting I don't like the way you're treated."

Kylie waited for a minute. When Filer didn't say anything else she knew he'd given her permission without saying anything. When neither of her parents said no Kylie said, "Jeffery is coming to pick me up so we can 'run lines' for the show."

Chapter 28

In a run-down ranch house on the edge of Pacific Palisades Jeffery said to his agent, "I'm picking her up this evening. We're going to run lines." Jeffery made the phrase run lines sound like something out of a porn movie.

"Go easy on her. I think we've got something with her. You and the perv have run off some of the best guest actresses. No one will come near the show."

"Not my fault. It's good ole American Daddy who's all over them. And the writers think we can get away with anything as long as we get the laughs."

"You won't be laughing if one of these bimbos decides they can make more money suing the show instead of acting."

"Relax. This girl is straight off the farm. She'll do anything to stay on the show."

"Well pass the word on to Larry. Tell him he's heading to a court date if he doesn't tone down his bad habits."

"What do you mean?"

"No more of the lingering feel-ups on set when everyone else has to play it straight. No peaking in the female dressing room. Keep him away from Kylie-period."

"You should be talking to Larry. Jesus, he's supposed to be the adult on the show."

Tery cautioned Jeffery, "Remember we had this conversation and take it as a warning not to go along with him-understand!"

"Okay Tery, I get it. It's been nice talking to you. I've got to go to McLane's place to pick-up Kylie."

Chapter 29

Filer called Ted and they met up at the Bistro.

Both men ordered beers and sat down by the arched window.

Filer explained he'd decided to go ahead with the interview.

"Okay," Ted said, "I've got something for you to take along for the interview."

"What would that be?" Filer asked. "I've got a resume."

Ted showed Filer a strange coin. It looked like a casino token, but when Filer examined it up close it had Ted's army unit on one side and a picture of a bridge builder with the words Operating Engineer inscribed below it.

"I still don't know what this is," Filer said.

"Give it to Cochrane when you do the interview and say that Ted says hi. He'll know what the coin is for."

"You're not going to tell me what the coin is are you?"

"You should find that out on your own."

Filer put the coin in his pocket and finished drinking his beer.

Chapter 30

Cliff, Steve Williams' brother, had a job in L.A. as a used car salesman. He didn't have much of a life. He knew he was lucky to have a job. Until he finished his parole he had to stay near his parole officer and make weekly reports.

Cliff spent his off hours at a local sports bar. The sports bar had three TVs; one behind the bar and one at either end of the bar.

Cliff mainly went to the sports bar so he didn't have to sit at home alone. His parole officer probably wouldn't like the company Cliff kept in the bar, but he had a big case load and as long as Cliff reported in each week his parole officer considered Cliff one of the good ones.

One night just before Cliff was going to leave the bar for home he saw a commercial that caught his attention. There on the screen a man appeared Cliff thought he'd left behind years ago. Mad Dog Wilson, the man who backed his brother down in front of a line crew was letting a woman throw him to a mat. He watched a minute longer to make sure it was Mad Dog and then he left the bar.

Steve Williams kept in touch with Cliff by calling from prison. The next day when Steve called he told him what he'd seen.

"You're not going to believe this."

"Come on Cliff. Don't fuck around."

"Remember that Mad Dog character on the line crew in Oregon?"

"Yeah, yeah I remember-so what?"

"He's here in L.A."

"What?"

"Yeah, I saw him in a commercial on TV."

Cliff waited for his brother to say something. "You okay Steve?"

"I'll tell you next time you call."

Chapter 31

Filer's gaze followed the steel frame towers that marched along-side the highway. He had spent some good years working as a line man and if he didn't count being electrocuted he figured he'd gained more than he lost. He had Abbey and Kylie as family now. They were a result of the nomadic life of a lineman. But now he needed another kind of life so he could stay close to home and family. The life of a boomer wasn't how he wanted to continue.

Maybe if he switched back to being a heavy equipment operator he could get the kind of quality time he wanted with his family.

Would he miss hiking his butt up poles all day long? He doubted it. And the truth was-he didn't hike up poles much anymore. On steel work he climbed up the towers with no need for spikes. He hadn't used his spikes for a couple of years. Of course it was like riding a bicycle. If you spent ten years climbing the wooden poles it wasn't something you forgot.

On the long stretch across Nevada Filer's thoughts went back to *American Daddy.* He didn't like the show. He didn't like the actors, especially the young punk playing the son. He didn't like the character he played, and he didn't think the real person was much different than the character. He was glad Kylie only had the one time walk-on. If he saw the punk off the show around Kylie he would set him straight about a real father figure.

Maybe he should buy a couple of books on philosophy or religion Filer thought. These long drives would be the perfect place to think about both subjects. Of course he'd have to keep his mind on the driving, but there probably wasn't a person alive who could keep stray thoughts from popping up on this drive.

Take road signs for instance-if there would be a law against stray thoughts all of the road signs should come down. Who wouldn't think of the next gas station in twenty miles, or the next road side attraction?

At the mentioned road side attraction Filer pulled into the parking lot beside the gas pumps. He got out and the attendant hurried out to ask Filer, "Fill'er up?' Filer nodded and the attendant put the gas pump nozzle in the tank and started washing the windshield.

Filer came back from the rest room and the attendant asked if he wanted the oil checked.

"No, I just checked it."

With the pump on ten dollars it shut off and Filer handed the attendant a ten dollar bill.

Back on the road Filer gave a little thought to what questions he'd be asked in the interview. Number one, he thought, would be why he was giving up line work.

Easy answer; he'd given it a lot of thought. "Line work was getting harder to find. Next question: "Can you move here to do this job?"

"I'm a boomer, always have been. At least I'll be a little closer to family with this job."

"Are you a team player?"

"People get along with me. I get along with them."

In Filer's mind the interviewer gave him the eye after that answer.

"I'm a working man. Construction work isn't a church social. Someone pounds on you, you pound back. But there is the golden rule: do to others as they do to you-only do it first. I'd better not put that one in," Filer thought.

Filer didn't think he'd have any trouble in the interview. He was a heavy equipment operator who had taken a vacation, well a long vacation, by going into line work.

It got dark and Filer figured he was close to Winnemucca. It felt good to be out of the desert. He took the first exit into Winnemucca and stopped at a Motel 6. After a quick check-in Filer went to the adjoining casino for dinner. He didn't feel like gambling. He'd save his luck for the interview. Filer called Abbey from his motel room and checked in. It was a ritual after many years spent on the road. She asked how the trip had been. Filer told her it was a good drive with no problems.

Chapter 32

After a good night's sleep Filer woke up and told the desk clerk he was up and didn't need the wake-up call.

Filer arrived at the Pegasus Co. office fifteen minutes early. Better to sit awhile in a reception room than be late.

Denise, an attractive brunette, and Cochrane's Administrative Assistant, greeted Filer and told him Cochrane would see him on time. She offered Filer a seat and turned back to some business on her desk.

The full fifteen minutes passed and Denise said, "Mr. Wilson, Mr. Cochrane is ready for you. You can go on in."

Bruce Cochrane motioned Filer to a chair in front of his desk.

"Welcome to Winnemucca Mr. Wilson."

Filer nodded. Sitting in front of Cochrane's desk the first thing Filer noticed was a mining safety award on his desk. The second thing he saw was a built in trophy case with its glass shelves filled with golfing trophies. And sitting in a corner of the office there was a golf bag filled with golf clubs.

Filer put his attention back on the man with his resume in his hand.

"This might not be the right time to give you this," Filer said. Then he took the strange coin out of his shirt pocket and put it on Cochrane's desk. After having thought about it on the trip up from California Filer thought the coin might be a kind of Masonic thing.

Cochrane picked up the coin and turned it over in his hand. "Ted said you should give me this coin?"

"Yes, that's all he told me. He wouldn't tell me anything else."

Cochrane put the coin in his top desk drawer and said, "Okay I've got the coin." He looked Filer in the eyes and then went on with the interview.

"I have your resume here. The color photo is a nice touch. Well let's get started. This is Bill he'll be your foreman-if you're hired."

Cochrane smiled, "I think you can relax. On your resume you say you can run dozers, D10's and D11's; and you can drive a caterpillar 777D. We need an equipment operator who can also work as a driver. I think we need you.

One other thing I need to know-do you golf?"

This statement shouldn't have surprised Filer with all of the golf gear in the office, but it did because he wasn't management. It wasn't like he partied with big bosses on a regular basis.

"No, I'm not a golfer."

"Hell," Cochrane said. "Are you sure?" Have you ever played miniature golf?"

It was a stretch, but Filer remembered going to a miniature golf course on a couple of dates in High School.

"I took a couple of dates in High School to a miniature golf course."

Cochrane smiled again." That's what I needed to hear. Okay Mr. Wilson welcome aboard; you're hired.

Bill is going to take you around the operation and drop you off at the personnel office to sign some papers."

Filer thought this strange interview was over, then Cochrane said, "One last thing- we're going to need you on our team for a golf Scramble this week end."

One again Filer didn't know what to think. "I don't have any golf clubs," he finally said.

"Don't worry about that; we have everything you need. We just need you to show-up here Saturday morning ready to go."

"I can do that," Filer answered.

"Okay, great," Cochrane said. "Bill is going to take you now. See you Saturday morning."

Chapter 33

Filer took a wake-up call from the front desk. The receptionist sounded almost as enthusiastic as Filer felt. It was 6:30, enough time to get cleaned up and grab a breakfast at the diner across the street. Then he'd be driving to Pegasus headquarters. From there he'd see how the day played out.

With a cup of coffee in hand Filer guided his pick-up onto the highway. Driving always was a time for his best thoughts. This morning his thoughts were on his wife and daughter. He wished they were with him. But Abbey had never been a stay at home mom, and Kylie-well she was very independent. That might be his fault. He always encouraged Kylie to stand up for herself.

His next thought was about what the day ahead would be like. He had to meet new people and learn how to play golf on a regular golf course-no clowns allowed.

With his thoughts keeping him occupied it didn't seem like long before he pulled into the Pegasus Company parking lot.

"Here goes. I'm off to see the wizard," Filer said to himself.

Inside the company office Denise smiled at Filer. "Mr. Mad Dog, everyone is in the meeting hall. Just follow the hallway straight back and go through the double doors. Filer smiled back at Denise. She wasn't the first woman to give him the business. Abbey had captured him by being outgoing and willing to take a chance on a boomer.

The hall was filled with men. Filer assumed they were Pegasus employees. He walked to a long table on one side of the hall and found his name tag. He saw Cochrane sitting at a front table and took a seat at that table.

"Morning Filer, I see you're on time. I like that in a new employee. These men will be on our team today. He made introductions: he gestured to a tall man on his right side. This is Buddha, he's a truck driver. Buddha nodded to Filer. He motioned to the next man and introduced him. This is Chuy; he's also a driver. And this is Ray; he's a loader operator. I expect you to keep him busy when you get to the job site. Ray won't be on our team today. I'm putting you on my top team. Don't let me down Filer."

After he made the introductions Cochrane got up and went to the podium at the front of the hall.

"Welcome to this year's Scramble. You've all been assigned to teams. We'll be playing the first nine holes on a closed course at the Municipal Golf Course. If this is your first time playing listen to the team leaders; they all know the rules. We'll have prizes for the best team score, and there will be a company lunch at the club house for everyone after the Scramble.

All right men this is a team building activity. If you're on a team with someone you don't know take the opportunity to network." Cochrane laughs. "Yeah, I said network. People may think you're just dumb miners but don't kid yourselves. It never hurts to make new friends.

Okay everyone let's get to the golf course. Drive safely and I'll see you at the Scramble."

Chapter 34

Cochrane came back to the table and asked if anyone needed a ride to the golf course.

Filer said, "I'd like to follow someone there."

"Okay, follow me. I'll be in the blue Blazer."

Filer walked beside Cochrane to the parking lot.

Following the convoy of vehicles, Filer thought of his father's funeral. Just seven years earlier Clayton Wilson died of an aneurism. He died young, only fifty-two years old. Filer was sorry to have lost his dad. He felt like they had the best years ahead of them. He had been truly close to Clayton Wilson. Having Abbey, Kylie and Maggie, his mother helped, but wasn't the same as having Clayton.

Ahead of him, the Blazer made a turn and Filer turned behind it. He followed the Blazer to a tree covered acreage that stood out in the surrounding desert environment. Cars and pick-ups started filling the parking lot around the Municipal Golf Course. Filer pulled in beside the Blazer and got out to accompany Cochrane to the club house. A long line of golf carts with canvas shade canopies were parked, waiting for the Scramble to begin.

Men were hauling coolers out of their vehicles and loading them into the golf carts.

Chuckling to himself, Filer saw men dressed in knee length golfing knickers and spikey golf shoes. Most of the men were in their everyday t-shirts, shorts and tennis shoes. Thirty-six men in four man teams made up nine teams.

Cochrane disappeared into the club house and came out with a golf bag with nine clubs in it and gave the bag to Filer.

"This is your basic set of clubs. Once we get to the first tee we'll tell you which club to use. Don't worry about anything." Cochrane could tell Filer was a little nervous. "We're here to have a lot of fun."

Cochrane handed Buddha a sheet that showed which teams were assigned to which fairways. Their team was assigned to the first fairway.

On the first tee, Cochrane teed off first. He made a straight shot down the fairway. Buddha teed off next. Not the shot Cochrane had made but on the fairway. Chuy stepped up to the tee, a little nervous; Filer thought. Chuy adjusted his stance and drew back his club. When Chuy followed through with his swing, the ball took a wide flight to the left and into the rough. Chuy backed off of the tee with a disappointed frown.

"Okay Filer, my man, it's your shot."

Cochrane handed Filer a driver out of the rental bag. Filer took the club and tried to walk to the ball with confidence. He approached the tee box and put his ball on a plastic tee.

"Don't try to smash it. If you baby it off the tee we won't laugh," Buddha said.

"Just look down the fairway and imagine that's where your ball is going," Cochrane advised. "It's kind of like mind over matter."

Filer straightened up and remembered how the other guys completed their swings.

"What the hell," Filer thought and let loose with a hell bent for leather swing.

"At least he didn't miss the ball," Cochrane said.

The ball sailed down the fairway and landed ten feet behind Cochrane's ball.

"Hey Buddha," Cochrane said. "It looks like we've got a natural here."

The rest of the team members patted Filer on the shoulders. Filer had a little smile as he walked off the tee box toward the golf cart.

Cochrane opened the cooler and the team members took beers or sodas. Filer noticed that Buddha took a coke. Cochrane grabbed a Bud so Filer felt comfortable taking a Bud.

Sipping their drinks, Cochrane's team rolled down the fairway in two golf carts, picking up short shots and Chuy's ball from the rough until they got to Filer's shot. Filer's shot was a little short of Cochrane's shot, but it had a better lie. According to Scramble rules the team would play forward from his position.

"Way to go Filer," Chuy congratulated Filer.

"Call me Mad Dog," Filer said smiling out from his Fu Manchu. Filer felt like he'd done pretty well for being on the golf course the first time.

"This is a par three hole," Cochrane explained to Filer as he took his shot. As usual he hit a straight shot down the fairway. Buddha pulled to the left again; Chuy landed just in the rough; and Filer made another fairly straight shot landing further than his last shot from Cochrane. The team played forward from Cochrane's lie. Filer saw Cochrane keeping count of their strokes. After he totaled up the strokes it was Chuy's turn to putt on the third green.

Filer could guess from Chuy's expression that the whole golf thing was not his bag.

Chuy squared off on the green and sighted to the cup. He has a ten foot putt to keep the team three over par. If he misses they will be four or five strokes over par. Chuy sighted from the ball to the cup again and brings back his putter. The other team members are still waiting to see where the ball will go. Chuy putted the ball and it rimed the cup without going in and stopped a foot and a half past the cup. The other team members let out a collective breath as Chuy tapped the ball into the cup.

Filer has watched golf on T.V. while channel flipping; and he has seen the crowd hushed when golf pros preform on the green. Now he can appreciate the whole golf thing. He hasn't had to putt yet.

The team parked their golf carts by the sixth hole. Filer 'Mad Dog' Wilson's luck has run out. On this tee he duffs the ball and it bounces fifty yards down the fairway.

"How in the hell did that happen?" Filer wondered. "I was doing so good." Off of this tee it is Buddha's turn to shine. His swing is perfect and he even hits the ball past Cochrane's shot. Even Chuy stays on the fairway; and they all load back into the golf carts.

"Don't take it so hard Mad Dog," Chuy says, "Beginner's luck has to run out sometime."

They all sipped on their drinks as Cochrane steered the golf cart down the fairway. On the whole, Cochrane is happy. The team is only four strokes over par.

On the seventh hole everyone gets off decent shots. Filer's shot is only average, but better than his last shot. Filer hasn't putted yet but he knows according to Scramble rules he'll have to putt at least once. The team gets on the green and their only chance to stay at a four over par is for Cochrane, their best putter, to take the shot.

Cochrane lines up his shot and makes the putt. The ball rolls sweetly into the cup.

The eighth hole goes about the same as the seventh hole, and Buddha makes the putt. With only the ninth hole left Filer sees the writing on the club house wall-he'll be the one to putt. It's been fun up to now, not much pressure and a couple of beers to settle the nerves.

On the ninth hole, out of nowhere, Cochrane hooked his drive and lands his ball in the rough. Filer again rolls a ball fifty yards down the fairway. Chuy and Buddha make good drives down the fairway.

With the next round of play Cochrane comes back with a straight shot half way to the green. Buddha and Chuy make good shots with good lies and Filer's luck stays bad. He comes in behind the other three.

Now Cochrane takes a money shot onto the green circle. Chuy also lands on the green; and Buddha lands outside the green.

All the team looks at Filer as they get into the golf carts. He knows it is finally his turn on the green. This putt could have been a no pressure situation if they were under par but they aren't under par.

To have a chance at winning Filer has to make the putt in one stroke. And luck doesn't seem to be on his side. It is still his turn to putt, so he decides to have a little fun. They have dragged him out here-a complete amateur, to fill out the foursome. He is the dark horse in this deal and knows Cochrane has to pay him no matter how the putt turns out. He also has the full time job no matter how the Scramble turns out.

His three team mates are leaning on golf clubs as Filer takes a putter from Cochrane.

As he thinks the putt over he can baby the ball in by taking a couple of weak strokes, or he can go for the hero shot and try to make the putt in one stroke. This strategy actually combines both options-if he misses he'll still have to take a couple of shots to get the ball in. Might as well go for the gold Filer decides.

So now, to give the boys a show Filer gets behind the ball and sights across the green toward the cup. He can see the swells and rises between the ball and the cup. The shot will take a little finesse. If he hasn't used up all of his beginner's luck he just might make it.

Filer stands up beside the ball and draws back his club. He hits the ball and watches it roll slowly but steadily toward the cup. Will he be the hero or the goat? The ball hits the cup and titters around the rim. Filer draws a breath and doesn't think the putt is going to fall in. Then the ball tips in and he hears Cochrane clapping his hands.

"Way to go Mad Dog. I knew I hired you for a good reason."

Filer climbs into the golf cart with the rest of the team smiling at him.

"You're okay, Mad Dog," Buddha says.

At the Scramble after party Cochrane made a big deal over the Scramble. The party was catered with grilled steaks, burgers, hot dogs, and kegs of beer.

There were trophies for teams and individual trophies. Filer accepted a Beginners Luck trophy for his final putt.

After the awards were given out Cochrane gave Filer a brief explanation of the job he would be doing.

After drinking a couple of beers Filer asked Cochrane, "What was the coin all about?"

Cochrane looked at Filer and said, "It is part of the game Mad Dog. Did Ted tell you the story about the Green Berets?"

"Yeah he told me he rebuilt a bridge for them."

"I'll tell you this. It's a challenge coin. You'll have to find out the rest for yourself."

After more celebrating with Cochrane and his Scramble team Filer made the drive back to L.A. to get his trailer.

Chapter 35

Now, when Steve Williams watched TV he couldn't forget what his brother Cliff had told him about Filer 'Mad Dog' Wilson being in a commercial. Filer became the first man on his list of men he had to settle a score with. He thought of revenge 24/7. It was only a little more difficult since he was behind bars.

Williams' problem, as he thought of it, divided in two parts-finding someone on the outside to do what he wanted and how to pay the hitman for doing the job.

Solving the second part of the problem gave him the solution to the first part of the problem.

Steve Williams became a member of the Brotherhood. As a member he got a prison job. But he also had to give sixty percent of his prison salary to the leader of the Brotherhood. In return for the money pledge the Brotherhood gave him a contact number for the favor he wanted done on the outside.

On his weekly call Steve spoke to Cliff, "I'm going to give you a name and address and I want you to contact the man and tell him I want Filer 'Mad Dog' Wilson dead."

"I can't Stevie, I just got out of jail and I'm on probation."

"Don't call me that, (Williams hated his childhood nickname) and I want it done. Just think of all the times I took care of you as a kid."

Cliff thought back to Steve getting him out of the house when their old man came home drunk and needed someone to take his frustrations out on. They had been lucky when their father ran his pickup truck into a semi and died on the spot. Then their mother had to get another job and Steve took care of Cliff full time. Now Cliff owed Steve. Steve knew it and took advantage of Cliff on a regular basis.

"Okay," Cliff said. "Give me the name and address."

Chapter 36

Cliff entered one of the worst neighbor hoods in L.A. and drove until he found the address Steve had given him. Fearing the worst he walked from his parked car to the front door of a deteriorating bungalow and knocked on the door.

The door opened and a heavily tattooed middle-aged white man answered the door.

"Yeah."

Cliff explained who had sent him and gave him a phone number to verify that Cliff had contacted him and that he understood the message.

The tattooed man shut the door in Cliff's face. Cliff figured he'd done his job and retreated to his car.

Chapter 37

Abbey and Kylie were having dinner after staying late at the *American Daddy* set. Kylie spoke to Abbey over dessert. "Jeffery wants to go to San Francisco next week-end. There's a big party there. All of his friends are going and I really want to go."

"Kylie, you're a grown woman. I don't think it's a good idea, but I'm not going to say no. Just be very careful. By now you know what Jeffery and Larry are like. They're not just that way on the set."

"I'm sure Jeffery loves me. I trust him."

"I know you do. Just be careful baby."

The two women finished dessert in a mutually agreed on silence.

Chapter 38

With the meal almost over there was a knock at the carriage house door. Kylie got up from the dinner table and went to the door.

"Kylie, turn on your TV and switch to channel 50. You've got to see this," Sharon Farris, one of Kylie's friends said.

Kylie turned on the TV in the living room and switched the TV to channel 50. The TV came on in the middle of Dyna Rees' Dynamo Dojo for Women commercial.

Dyna had just pinned Filer to the mat and was keeping him there with a leg over the chest arm bar hold.

"Mom, you've got to see this," Kylie yelled to Abbey.

Abbey came into the living room and saw her husband Filer putting his arm around another woman. The move would be part of Dyna's escape move from an arm lock strangle hold.

Abbey and Kylie watched the three minute commercial filled with Filer interacting with Dyna.

When the commercial was over Abbey didn't know what to think or say. She would have to wait until she could talk to Filer. Abbey assured herself there was a good reason for Filer doing the commercial. What she couldn't understand was why he hadn't told her about it before making the commercial.

Chapter 39

On the drive back to California Filer was beginning to feel like an over the road trucker. The only consolation to the drive could be the scenic drive on 101along the Pacific coast he planned to take back to Los Angeles. The alternative route through Bishop had cut about 6 hours off the trip on the way up, but he wanted a little more time to think on the way back.

Filer loaded his pick-up, but at the last moment after looking at his map he decided to skip the 101 and save the trip for when he could make it with Abbey and Kylie. He would return to Los Angeles through Bishop and cut the six hours off the trip. This way would still take eight hours with plenty of time to think of the future.

On the road Filer started to think of the next six months. As it had been explained to him the reclaim job would last six to eight months. At the end of the reclaim he could talk to Cochrane about a full time job with Pegasus.

The reclaim wouldn't be like mining work even if it involved working on mining property. The goal of the reclaim would be to restore the property as much as possible to the way it was before the company started mining the land.

Filer watched the sun traveling across the sky from being in his eyes to shining off to his right. His life had involved a lot of traveling to and from jobs for the last ten years. Some people had nine to five jobs. He'd had a nine to five job himself back when he worked for the county. It had seemed boring back then; now he could appreciate boring. He'd had his fill of the long hours on the road and being away from family and friends.

The last months being in Hollywood were confusing. *The Copper Thieves* movie made him into somewhat of a hero. Not the main hero of the book, but a hero to those around him. The actor playing him was a little taller and thinner, just the same he was a little stronger. The book made him clever and he got some good lines in the movie. Did he now have a reputation to live up to? He was a working man with a working man's morals and ethics. Would he be laughed at if his friends and work mates could hear his thoughts? He might not say the words but he had an image to live up to.

Filer drove out of Nevada and came into California through Bishop.

Later Filer could see the light of Los Angeles. "Thank God," Filer thought. "I've had enough alone thinking time for a while."

Filer would be overnight in Malibu and then he'd be back on the road with his trailer to Winnemucca; not much turn-around time.

When Filer parked his Chevy outside the carriage house he could see Abbey's car wasn't in the driveway. He had wanted to see her when he got back, but his homecoming wasn't going to be like he imagined it.

Inside the carriage house Abbey had left a note. "Sorry Filer, Kylie is working late at the studio. I'll see you when we get home."

"Guess I'll see if Ted's got plans," Filer thought.

He dialed Ted's number and Ted picked up on the second ring.

"Ted, what's up? I'm back in town. Could you drink a beer and listen to my tall tale about the golf Scramble in Winnemucca?"

"Sure Mad Dog. Let's meet at the Bistro. It's close to your place. Do you know it?"

"Yeah, I know it. I've been there with Abbey a couple of times."

"Okay amigo, I'll see you there in half an hour."

Filer cleaned up and put on clean clothes. He started to feel a little better about being back in California.

Chapter 40

Ted walked into the Bistro and spotted Filer sitting by a window set in a rounded arch overlooking the sidewalk. Filer gave him the high sign and Ted nodded back and walked to the table. Ted sat down and a waitress came to their table.

Filer ordered a Bud, and Ted wanted a Coors.

"Coming right up," the waitress acknowledged their orders.

"Glad to see you back in town," Ted said. "How did the interview go?"

"That's one crazy friend you've got," Filer said. "He hired me to play in a golf Scramble."

Ted didn't say anything and waited for Filer to continue.

"Cochrane asked me all the right questions about construction and then he wanted to know if I'd ever played golf."

"Well that sounds like Cochrane. He's not one to let work get in the way of playing golf. So how did you do?"

"Do you mean did I get the job, or how did I do on the golf course?"

"Did you get the job?"

"I want to know if the coin had anything to do with getting the job."

Ted said, "It probably didn't hurt, but you got the job didn't you?"

"I got the job and I'm heading back to Winnemucca tomorrow."

"That doesn't give you much turn-around time."

"The job is a reclaim job and it's on a timeline. I told Cochrane I could work under pressure and I guess that means I have to hustle back."

"And...," Ted asks, smiling, "How did you do on the golf course?"

"To tell you the truth I still don't really understand how a golf Scramble

97

works, but I made the last putt of the game. It must have been important because Cochrane called me a natural."

"Sounds like you made a friend; if you don't mistake a boss for a drinking buddy. Off of the golf course Cochrane is all business."

"I kind've got that idea when Cochrane was explaining the reclaim job and the deadline. He said if the reclaim was finished on time there is a good chance he can get me on permanent with Pegasus."

Ted sipped his beer and glanced out the window, then looked back at Filer. "You know I think I could get you on permanent here as a gaffer if you wanted it."

"No thanks Ted. I'm a heavy equipment operator. Hollywood's not my thing."

"You never know unless you try. But just remember I can get you on if you ever need a job."

"Thanks. I'll keep that in mind."

Ted noticed Filer staring over his shoulder. "What's up? You look like you've seen a ghost."

"What's that?" Filer asked.

"What're you looking at?"

"Well, I don't know for sure. Since I made that commercial I keep thinking someone's following me-staring at me. Whenever I try to catch someone staring they disappear."

"Ted said, "Now that you've had your fifteen minutes of fame you're a public figure. Probably a lot of people stare at you and try to figure out where they've seen you before."

"That sounds about right. But it's still a little spooky."

"You'll get used to it. Haven't you had an old line hand come up and call you by name?"

"Yeah that's happened. It's embarrassing as hell."

"On the other hand just because you're paranoid doesn't mean someone isn't out to get you."

"I'll remember that," Filer said and smiled.

The two men sipped their beers and listened to Spanish music on the juke box.

"Have you talked to Abbey since you got back?"

"She wasn't home. She left a note saying she was with Kylie at the *American Daddy* studio."

Ted sat his beer down. He looked like he had something important to say but didn't know if he should say it.

Filer looked at Ted. "What is it?"

"There's a rumor that Kylie is up for a big part because she's Lodder's girlfriend."

"Isn't that how they do things in this town?" Filer asked.

"Yeah, but Lodder has a very bad reputation. He doesn't do favors for nothing."

"Abbey's been around. She's helping Kylie. She can handle it."

"If Kylie's going to make it out here she's going to have to have a professional manager or an agent."

"I'll have to leave that to Abbey."

"You know Filer, managers are blood suckers. They'll take your money and leave you without a penny if you're not careful."

"Well Abbey will have to handle it. If that's what Kylie wants they'll have to figure it out."

"You should talk to Shane. As agents go he has a pretty good one."

"I'll tell Abbey. Speaking of, I'd getter get home."

Both men took a last drink of beer and left the Bistro together.

When Filer pulled into the carriage house drive way Abbey's car was parked there.

Inside the carriage house Abbey was awake watching TV. She heard Filer come into the living room.

"How did it go at the studio?" Filer asked.

"Kylie is doing really well for never having any acting experience."

Filer said, "I guess those school plays in elementary school don't count."

"Compared to real acting, no they don't count. Those plays were just little kids doing their thing."

"Do you think Kylie likes acting?" Filer asked.

"Yes, she is really into it. Being with Jeffery doesn't hurt," Abbey admitted.

"What about that boy? There are rumors he's a lot like his character on the show."

"Well the rumors aren't true." Abbey was quick to defend Jeffery.

"I'd keep an eye on him," Filer said. Then he added, "I don't want to leave you here, but I have to go to work."

Abbey touched Filer's shoulder. "This is a chance for Kylie to make a career. You know I have to stay with her."

"I didn't say anything," Filer protested. "Ted said you should talk to Shane and see if he'll set you up with his agent."

Abbey kissed Filer and said, "That's a really good idea, Mad Dog." She called him Mad Dog in intimate circumstances.

"I have a good idea every once in a while," Filer said. Abbey smiled at him.

Abbey took Filer's hand and led him into the bedroom.

According to the way Abbey was acting Filer knew she was after something.

After sex and some cuddling Abbey asked Filer, "Sweetie who is Dyna Rees, and why did you do that commercial without telling me?"

Filer hesitated for a minute getting his thoughts in order. "Dyna Rees owns Dynamo Dojo for Women and she hired me to do the commercial. Well she didn't hire me. Shane and Chet, Shane's manager, got me an interview with Earnie Beckford. I didn't know what the commercial would be, or who would be in it until after Earnie hired me."

Abbey was giving Filer her full attention. "Why didn't you tell me?"

"I wanted it to be a surprise. You and Kylie are doing a lot I don't know about. So I wanted it to be a surprise."

"Well you sure got that part right," Abbey said.

"Don't you want to know why I did it?"

Abbey looked puzzled and then asked, "Why did you do it?"

"Shane got me the commercial so you and Kylie would have enough money to stay in Hollywood while she's working on *American Daddy*. The money from the commercial would pay the bills until I got my first pay check from construction work."

"What about Dyna Rees? She's a nice looking woman."

"Dyna's single, but Dynamo Dojo is her thing."

"Are you going to do another commercial?"

"Earnie said he'd call me if he got something." Filer bragged a little, "Earnie said I'm a natural. The camera loves me."

Abbey laughed.

Filer and Abbey made love again and then went to sleep.

Chapter 41

Filer woke up before Abbey and he didn't wake her up. He showered, dressed and went to the kitchen. It was easy enough to make coffee. He sat down with his first cup and was sipping it when Abbey came into the kitchen. She poured herself a cup of coffee and smiled at Filer.

"What do you want for breakfast," Abbey asked smiling.

"Whatever you're cooking," Filer said and smiled.

While he waited for breakfast Filer set food and water out for Girlfriend. She had been rubbing against his ankles until he noticed her.

"I guess the only member of the Wilson family coming with me will be Girlfriend," Filer joked aloud.

Abbey gave Filer a guilty look. "You know I have to stay here with Kylie. She needs me; at least for a little while."

"I know," Filer replied. "You don't have to convince me. If Shane's agent takes her on as a client that will help won't it?"

"I'm not talking about money. I'm talking about making sure she has a regular home life. She didn't go to college so I don't think she's ready to be on her own yet."

Filer thought about his own life. After high school he went to heavy equipment school, received the equivalent of an associates' degree, and then into the Seabees. He had grown up a lot in Vietnam.

When he got back to the states he made a life for himself first as an equipment operator and then as a lineman. That's when he met Abbey and Kylie. He dated Abbey, they married and he adopted Kylie. They had made a father and daughter bond. But now they were growing apart. "Speak of the devil," Filer thought. Kylie came into the kitchen wearing a blouse with a pair of short shorts Filer didn't care for; a California thing that she took up not long after they came to California.

"Congratulations," Filer said, not sure he believed her new career was something he should be congratulating her for.

Kylie looked his way and gave him a little smile, "I guess I'm not the only one with the acting bug."

Filer smiled back, "I don't know about that."

"Are you going to do more commercials?"

"I'm still going back to construction work. I got a job in Winnemucca."

"So you'll be going to live in Winnemucca. How long will you be gone this time?"

"This job is different. If I get on with Pegasus it will be like a nine to five job." Filer smiled and said, "More like a ten hour day rather than an eight hour day. We could buy a house there. You and your mother could move to Nevada."

Kylie looked at Filer like she did when he first moved in with her and Abbey. "I can't go. I'm going to be an actor on *American Daddy.*"

Abbey looked at Filer and then turned her eyes down.

Filer knew there was no chance they would be coming to Winnemucca.

Filer helped Girlfriend into her carrier and sat it down beside the door.

"Good," Kylie said. "That cat hates Jeffery. If she could have gotten close to him she would have scratched him."

Chapter 42

"Girlfriend is a good judge of character. She doesn't make many mistakes."

Kylie said, "Still I'm glad she's going with you."

"Keep an eye on this guy Kylie." Filer explained what Ted had told him about Jeffery, and about the *American Daddy* program.

"That's just show business gossip dad. No one ever says anything good about anyone else."

"Well you and your mother will have to take care of Hollywood. I have to make a living."

Filer picked up the cat carrier and left the kitchen. Abbey walked with him to the front door.

"Don't worry about Kylie. We'll be okay. Stay safe Filer," Abbey said and kissed him before he went out the door.

"Well Girlfriend, all of this back and forth driving is getting a little old. At least this time I'll have company."

Filer put Girlfriend on the front seat. She had already curled up for a nap.

"I guess you won't be talking my ear off," Filer thought.

Chapter 43

Later in Winnemucca, Filer backed his trailer into the lot Pegasus' HR department had arranged for him. He was too tired to do any of the hook ups so he and Girlfriend would have to go to sleep when the sun went down. He could go for takeout and he had bread and cold cuts in a cooler.

For the time being Girlfriend would have to stay inside. He would let her out when he could watch her and be there when she wanted back in. He had full confidence she could take care of herself; he just wanted to make sure how safe the neighborhood was before he left her on her own. It's funny, he thought, that's almost the same way he felt about Kylie.

It was Sunday night and he had Monday to get the trailer set up and hooked into power, sewer, and phone services.

Filer ate his sandwich with the last light of the day. Girlfriend ate her cat food and settled in for the night.

Chapter 44

At six o'clock Filer woke up to a knock on the door. He lay still for a minute making sure of what he'd heard. "Yes," he thought someone is knocking on the door. He got out of bed and put on sweat pants and a T-shirt. He opened the door and was face to face with a middle aged woman.

"Hi, my name is Jane. You know like in Jane Doe."

"Morning," Filer managed to get out.

Jane handed him a cardboard container with a coffee and an egg Mac Muffin in it.

"Hope Mikey D is ok with you."

"Yeah, sure," Filer said.

"Well I'm here to help you get set-up. You'll have to do the hard stuff. You know, hook up the sewer line and the electrical, but I'll call in the utilities and the phone company. Leave me your keys and I'll be here to let the service people in."

"I've got the day off," Filer got in.

"Good for you," Jane said.

Just then Girlfriend came into the living room and curled around Filer's ankles.

"I see you've got an animal."

"This is Girlfriend," Filer introduced the Siamese to Jane.

"That's an unusual name," Jane said.

"That's only one of her names. She also answers to Her Majesty and Kitty."

"Let me give you a little advice. We have coyotes out here in the desert and family pets are like fast food to coyotes. You should keep her indoors as much as possible."

Filer gave a half smile. "I'll keep that in mind. Thanks for the breakfast."

Jane tipped a hand to her forehead and climbed into her jeep. Filer was left with the fast food breakfast and Girlfriend wanting her bowl filled with cat food.

"Looks like you'll be staying inside for a while," Filer said to the cat as he filled her bowl.

Filer put on work clothes and started making the necessary connections to the trailer park hook ups. It took him an hour to do the hook-ups. He still didn't have a phone connection so he got in his pick-up and drove into Winnemucca to call Abbey and tell her everything was okay.

By the end of the day Filer was ready to go to work.

Chapter 45

Early Tuesday morning filer woke up with Girlfriend hogging the center of the bed, nothing new there. He fed Girlfriend and left for work.

Chapter 46

Shane talked Chet into taking Kylie on as her manager. Chet negotiated a good deal for her; and was looking forward to making some money off his new starlet. Their contract didn't last long.

Abbey replaced Chet as Kylie's manager: and she fired Jeffrey's agent, who had been representing Kylie. As Abbey saw it she understood Kylie better than Chet or the agent: and therefore represented her interests better than either of them. And now they were keeping Kylie's acting money in the family.

Chapter 47

At Pegasus Denise greeted Filer, "Good morning Mr. Wilson. What can we do for you?"

"I'm ready to go to work."

"Okay," Denise said and dialed Cochrane on the intercom. "Yes sir," Denise replied into the intercom. "Mr. Cochrane says for you to go in."

Filer walked to his new boss' door and went in.

"Hi there Filer, Ready to go to work?"

"Yeah, I'm ready."

"Denise will get a man here to drive you out where you can meet up with Buddha for a drive around. And don't worry today is a paid work day." Cochrane looked down at the papers on his desk.

Filer figured that was his cue to get out of the office. He left and stood in front of Denise's desk. Denise was finishing a call. "Someone will be here right away," she told Filer. Just then Bill, Filer's foreman came into the office.

"I need to speak to Cochrane for a minute."

Denise punched a button and then motioned the foreman into Cochrane's office. After he went in she told Filer to have a seat. A minute later Bill came out of Cochrane's office.

"Bill, Filer Wilson is riding with Buddha today. Can you make sure he gets to Buddha?"

"Sure," Bill said and smiled at Denise.

"Okay Mr. Wilson, Bill will take you to Buddha."

The two men walked out of the office together.

"Have you worked in mining before?" Bill asked.

"No, I haven't worked in mining, but I've got experience on most of the equipment I've seen here so far."

"Well for the time being Cochrane has you working on a reclaim crew. If you work out okay we'll see about getting you on permanent."

Filer nodded his head.

"You know Buddha is a sort of philosopher. He'll try to convert you if you're not careful. He's been around but he's also a good truck driver. He can run most of the equipment here at the mine. He's a good one to answer your questions while you're doing the ride along."

Filer nodded again.

Bill pulled up along-side the 777D Caterpillar Buddha was driving. Buddha stopped and Filer climbed up the passenger side of the truck. Bill waved at Buddha and drove away.

Chapter 48

"Welcome, Mr. Wilson," Buddha said. Filer settled into the passenger seat. A fat smiling Buddha sitting on the dashboard caught his attention. The small statue gave the truck cab a warm atmosphere.

The man driving the truck wore a brown hoodie over an orange t-shirt. He had a piece symbol pinned to the hoodie.

Buddha motioned out the window and said, "This land produced a million dollars' worth of gold ore. It's not like old time mining. The mining they do here is to get the smallest particles of gold. The gold is claimed by using chemicals. This is scientific mining."

"How long have you worked for Pegasus," Filer asked?

"I've been here five years. Pegasus is a good company. They pay on time and they give benefits."

Filer observed the land around the mining road. It was stepped in benches, and in some places test holes still remained. Reclaiming the land was the opposite of the mining process. Mountains of tailings were being moved to fill the mining tracks. In the end the property would be smoothed over to comply with EPA regulations.

Buddha spoke, "What do we do now Mad Dog? You've seen the site. We could play I spy, or maybe twenty questions."

Filer gave Buddha a questioning glance that said, "You're weird man."

"Are you a religious man Filer?"

"No, my parents weren't religious so I never went to church."

"Now we're getting somewhere. I'll tell you what I'm going to do. I'm going to explain Buddhism, and it will change your life."

Filer lounged back in the passenger seat. He never cared one way or the other about religion so listening to Buddha pass the time with a lecture on Buddhism wouldn't do any harm.

Buddha took a breath and started talking. "Buddhism isn't a religion as much as it's a philosophy high jacked by the Buddha's followers. Buddha told his disciples that he didn't want to be worshiped as a god but his followers had other ideas. In his lifetime Buddha lived the life of a prince followed by a life of study and discovery. He was born a prince, a nobleman with privileges. His father kept him isolated from the real world of common men and their suffering.

It wasn't until Buddha became a young man that his curiosity about the world outside the palace grounds caused him to enter the real world."

Buddha's words plus the monotony of the road ahead were making Filer sleepy. He just was able to resist dozing off. He grabbed a water bottle and took a sip of water.

"You following me my man," Buddha asked?

"Yeah, rich guy leaves the palace and finds a bunch of people who have a lot less than he does. So far I'm not identifying with the guy slumming it."

"Most people don't even follow that far. But think about Moses or Jesus Christ. Moses was a nobleman and Jesus was at least lower middle class."

"Okay, I'm here for the rest of the day if you're trying to make a point."

"Enough philosophy for today," Buddha said. "This job we're on now is the reverse of what mining is. Where the company dug pits to get at the gold we take waste and fill in the pits. When we're all done we use dozers and scrappers to smooth it all over. The EPA comes along behind and plants wildflowers"

"I believe what you said about Buddhism, but I can't accept that last part about the EPA planting wildflowers."

"Well wait and see," said Buddha pulling into the waste dump behind Chuy to wait for him to be loaded.

Chapter 49

"What's your story Filer?" "I was a lineman for fifteen years." Filer also knew Buddha wanted to Know about the Hollywood thing. "When I first started as an apprentice lineman I ran a crew with a murderer and a thief on it."

"How'd that turn out?"

"The murderer did okay as a grunt and a thief, but he wasn't much in the sociability department."

"So how did you end up in Hollywood?"

"Another grunt on the job wrote a book about the murder and made a big deal about me being the good guy and the other guys being bad guys. And during the same job we were on I got electrocuted while rescuing a pregnant woman."

"A big deal," Buddha said smiling.

"The grunt who wrote the book met a movie star I built a power line for in Montana, and they came up with the idea for the movie. We all got along really well so Shane McLane invited me to come to Hollywood with my family and work as a consultant. There you have the whole story."

"I'm guessing you don't like Hollywood."

"Nothing there is straight forward. Nobody tells you the truth without a lot of arm twisting. They think anything can be fixed with a couple of extra takes. Real life definitely isn't anything like that."

Buddha moved the truck forward to catch his next load.

Chapter 50

"You know in Buddhism there is sort of a second chance where a person who hasn't achieved Nirvana comes back to experience another lifetime on earth. No one calls cut and goes for another take, but there is karma. If you can avoid bad karma you can make up for past mistakes."

The truck thumped with the load dropped into its bed.

Buddha said, "If you think of it Mad Dog, except for a very few actions in our lives, the element of actions in the world around us are repetition after repetition of successful things we've learned to do to survive.

Think about it Mad Dog, when was the last time you did anything that was completely original-not related to anything you hadn't done before."

This line of thought took Filer by surprise. It really didn't make much difference, but he could see Buddha's point. He said, "What's so important about doing anything original?"

"Maybe the last original thing happened in the iron age when men smelted iron to make metal tools. Making bronze wasn't completely original, but it was a step forward. Men were started on a new path of adding more steps to the original idea of smelting metal."

"Okay gold is metal. I see that," said Filer.

"You're getting the idea."

"Splitting the atom was an original idea, but it took a lot of cooperation to do that. Atomic power wasn't even an entirely new idea because it used heat from splitting atoms to create steam that turns a turbine to make electricity."

"Filer asked, "Do you spend your time driving thinking this stuff up?"

"Wait and see," Buddha replied. "You have to think of something. This can be boring shit, back and forth, back and forth; even for twenty bucks and hour."

Buddha twisted the lid off of his thermos and poured himself a cup of coffee. He offered the thermos and a paper cup to Filer.

"I've got my own," Filer said and took out his thermos and poured himself a cup of coffee.

The two men drank coffee in silence and watched the scenery go by.

The rest of the ride along passed without much conversation and the two men returned to the Pegasus office.

Cochrane told Filer he would be running a dozer the next day. "Your foreman will drive you out to the site. He'll explain what you'll be doing and who you'll be working with.

Get a good night's sleep and we'll see you in the morning."

Filer got into his Chevy truck and drove back to his trailer.

Filer stopped at a K.F.C. on the way home and bought take out. He didn't feel like cooking. He was looking forward to seeing Girlfriend. It surprised him how much a part of his life she had become.

Chapter 51

Pulling his pickup in beside his trailer he glanced at the units on either side of his trailer. The trailer park catered to working class people. The park was even farther in distance to Winnemucca than its other suburbs. Sagebrush and Juniper bushes filled the desert land surrounding the trailer park.

Inside the trailer Girlfriend stood at the door anxiously waiting for Filer to let her go outside. Filer decided he didn't have much concern about coyotes getting the cat since she had survived on her own in a Montana trailer park until she finally decided to be a part of the Wilson family.

"Okay Girlfriend, be careful out there. I don't want you to be a snack for a starving coyote."

"Time for a shower," Filer said to himself.

Later as he sat in the trailer living room Filer saw a young couple pulling up to the trailer on his right. They looked like typical trailer park residents. The man wore a Levi jacket over a western shirt and Levis with cowboy boots. The woman wore a hooded sweatshirt with cotton slacks and flat shoes. She had bobbed brunette hair and pink lips. She carried a large purse over her shoulder.

The couple glanced at the red Chevy by Filer's trailer before going up wooden stairs into the trailer.

Filer didn't know how it happened but he already had a bad feeling from the man. It was probably the scowl on his face as he crossed their front yard.

Sitting the KFC box on the kitchen table Filer thought back to Maggie's fried chicken. He remembered the Fourth of July picnics at the park in Riverview. Nobody, not even KFC made fried chicken like Maggie. With Maggie on his mind after finishing the KFC take out Filer decided to call her.

First he had to see if Girlfriend was ready to come in. He opened the front door and whistled for the cat. Girlfriend came out from underneath the trailer, darted up the short stairway past him and into the kitchen where she knew her cat food would be waiting.

Chapter 52

Because he'd served in the military, and was married with an adopted daughter Filer didn't consider himself a momma's boy. As an only child he had developed close ties with both of his parents. When Clayton Wilson, his father, got in trouble, it was usually Maggie who had to put up with the consequences and aftermath. When Clayton died suddenly from an aneurism Filer had become closer to Maggie. Although he, Abbey and Kylie lived in another state they visited Maggie as often as possible, taking into consideration that they both worked and Kylie was in school. Now separated from Abbey and Kylie, Filer felt the need to talk with Maggie. It was seven o'clock and the phone rang three times before Filer heard Maggie saying hello.

"Hi mom, it's Filer. How are you doing?"

"Pretty much the same as always son."

Maggie sounded a little down. It was seven years since Clayton died and Filer knew Maggie missed him despite all the late nights he came in from drinking and hanging out at Stoney's bar in Riverview.

"How are you son?"

Filer couldn't help himself. He opened up. "Abbey and Kylie are in L.A. Kylie got a part in a sit-com called *American Daddy.* Abbey's staying with her to make sure she's doing okay."

"But how are you son?"

"Well, *The Copper Thieves* movie is wrapped up. That means its finished."

Maggie interrupted Filer. "I wasn't born yesterday Filer."

"Well since the movie is finished they don't need me as an advisor so I took a job at a gold mine in Winnemucca, Nev. I'll be operating a dozer again."

"I thought you were a lineman."

During the rest of the conversation Filer explained his decision to give up line work and go back to being a heavy equipment operator. Maggie said she thought he was making the right decision. She'd worried for him ever since he'd been electrocuted.

Filer ended the conversation by saying, "I love you mom."

"Love you son," Maggie replied.

Chapter 53

After dinner and a couple of TV programs Filer got ready for bed. He wasn't in bed long when he heard a moaning cry. It sounded like it was coming from his neighbor's trailer. Then Filer remembered he was now in the desert. It's probably a lonesome coyote. When he heard a second cry Girlfriend, A.K.A Kitty, ran into the bedroom and jumped onto the bed. She snuggled close, hoping for a session of being petted.

It's Filer's turn to sigh as he petted Girlfriend. Soon the sojourning duo were fast asleep.

In a dream Filer sees a coyote chasing Girlfriend. She is wearing a TV dinner box labeled Coyote Food. When the coyote catches Girlfriend she hisses and threatens the coyote with fangs and claws. The coyote yips and turns tail to disappear back into the desert.

Girlfriend squirmed and tried her best to hog half of the queen size bed. Filer woke briefly and thought, "Kitty, you are much more trouble than you're worth." In the morning over breakfast Filer apologized to Girlfriend. "Sorry about last night. You're good company." He chuckled to himself, "You're the only company I've got."

Chapter 54

At the show up Filer parked his truck and headed for the line-out room. He wasn't too worried because he was an equipment operator with on the job experience. Most of what there was to learn would be getting to know the rest of the operators. He already knew Buddha, who would be one of the truck drivers. He knew the foreman Bill, and he'd met a couple of the crew on the golf course. He told himself, "All you have to do is keep the dozer going! You've got good instincts and you can follow directions."

The line out room was filled with long folding tables and metal folding chairs. A side table held a twenty cup percolating coffee pot, with creams and sugars in small containers. Filer poured himself a coffee and sat down.

The rest of the crew soon filled the room. They drank coffee and stared at one another with the cocky confident attitude of having been on the job for months and some for years. One of the men looked Filer's way and had something to say to the man seated next to him. Both of the men laughed quietly waiting for the foreman to come into the room and line out their day.

Filer wasn't shy and knew soon enough he'd be telling jokes and laughing while he waited in this room.

Thinking back to what Buddha said Filer thought this type of work could be the same thing day after day and getting into a rhythm with the work helped get through the work day.

Bill stood up at a podium. He had a cup of coffee in one hand and a portable radio in the other. "Okay gentlemen we've got a new dozer operator. I don't know how good an operator he is, but I hear he's a hell of a golfer," Bill joked.

The crew who already knew Filer from the golf Scramble all laughed.

"Yeah he knows how to get a ball off the tee," Buddha laughed.

"He can putt a ball in a tight spot," Chuy added.

"Okay, okay, enough," Bill shut the group down. He was the one who made the jokes.

"We're working at the edge of the reclaim. Be careful of the amount of top soil you use out there to fill in the bare spots. We don't want to be making a bigger mess than there is already."

The crew got into the foreman's pickup for a ride to the site. The pickup bumped over a gravel road for twenty minutes and Filer watched the same route he'd been over with Buddha the day before. When Bill dropped off the crew he pulled Ray aside.

"Ray I want you to keep an eye on Filer. I'm sure he'll be fine, but keep an eye out just the same."

"Well, Filer, you heard what Bill said. I'm supposed to keep an eye on you. That sort of makes me lead man," Ray said with a straight face.

"Don't fuck up man," Chuy said. "You don't wanna see ole Ray when he gets a hard—on."

The crew kept silent for a half a minute and then they all broke up.

Filer made a serious face and then joined the rest of them laughing.

Filer thought about the new crew. "I'll have to fit in; but it's also like a jigsaw puzzle and it all has to be put together. Everyone will have to fit into the new puzzle. There will be corner pieces and side pieces; the easy parts of the puzzle to put together. It'll take a little bit of time to fill in the larger middle part of the puzzle. It just takes a little patience and time for everything and everybody to fit together."

Chapter 55

Filer climbed onto the D10 dozer and sat in the cushioned seat. Settled in, Filer thought of the reclaim scheme. The idea of the reclaim was to put the mined out land back as much as possible as it was before Pegasus had mined the land. The reclaim crew had already got more or less the contour of the land restored. Now the crew would be adding two feet of top soil to finish off the job. On his end of the job Filer would be using the dozer to keep the loader in business loading topsoil into trucks to be transported to the reclaim site.

Pegasus had an overall plan for the site before it started mining the area. Soil removed to get to the gold bearing oar was pushed aside and left in mounds. The gold ore was carried to slurry ponds to treat the ore so that ore finer than the smallest nuggets could be processed at the plant. Waste byproduct had to be treated so as not to be an environmental threat.

All of the steps of mining the gold were regulated by the EPA. The reclaim operation was the final step in the mining process.

It didn't take long for Filer to get back into the rhythm of the rumbling dozer. It took two to three minutes for the loader to fill a truck. Working at a forty five degree angle Filer shoved dirt to the loader. Buddha tipped his fingers in a salute to Filer as he pulled away from the loader. This small bit of recognition was enough to let Filer know he was doing his job the way it was supposed to be done.

As Filer settled into a routine on the reclaim job moments of thought turned to Abbey and Kylie in Hollywood. This wasn't the first time he'd been separated from them because of work. Line work meant being away from their home in Portland for months at a time. This time would be different because of Kylie's involvement with the Hollywood crowd. If it wasn't for her part in *American Daddy* maybe Filer could have talked Abbey into coming to Winnemucca to be with him.

Chapter 56

In Hollywood Kylie was developing a major crush on the boy/man star of *American Daddy*. Abbey was happy to see her daughter making a place for herself in the Hollywood scene, but she knew Kylie wasn't equipped to take care of herself. She was Portland, Oregon tough; this wasn't the same as being movie star tough. Because she attended Kylie's performances on a regular basis she knew the stars of *American Daddy* were bad actors-not in the sense of Hollywood acting but in the sense of grown adults who would do anything to get their own way. As much as she wanted to help Kylie she couldn't figure out how to keep Kylie from getting hurt by the male characters of *American Daddy*.

As much as Abbey couldn't help Kylie with her problem, after getting Filer's call and explanation about what was happening on the show Dyna Rees knew just what to do. When Kylie arrived at the Dynamo Dojo for Women Dyna instructed her on a couple of moves to make when Larry got handy on the set. The two women also talked about Filer.

Dyna explained how Filer was concerned for her safety on *American Daddy,* and that he wanted her to learn how to take care of herself at the dojo.

Chapter 57

Back in Winnemucca, Filer compared his first week back working as a dozer operator to the past years of working as a lineman. He was tired, but the aches and pains weren't the same as line work. Intellectually operating the dozer was less of a strain than figuring out the step by step building of steel towers. And the danger factors of line work out weighed working as an equipment operator.

Buddha invited Filer to a beer after work. After the foreman signaled an end to the work day Filer followed Buddha to a casino/restaurant in downtown Winnemucca. The men got a table and ordered dinner. Their waitress brought them beers to drink while they waited for their food.

"Well what do you think about the reclaim job?" Buddha asked.

"The main thing is that in line work I generally had more of a day to day deadline on work to be done. And I had more responsibility for getting the work done."

"Reclaim work is more relaxed than mining the ore and getting it to the processing operation," Buddha said.

"What do you have in mind for tomorrow," Buddha asked?

"Another day off at the trailer with Girlfriend," Filer replied.

"Want to have a little adventure?"

"It depends on the adventure," Filer answered.

"I thought you might want to talk to a real prospector. It won't take much time. You can be back here for a late lunch."

Filer thought over Buddha's invitation. "Okay, what time do we leave?"

"I'll pick you up at your place at nine o'clock. I'll bring a cup of coffee to get you woke up."

The two men drank their beers and then stopped at the slot machines for a couple of turns on the dollar machines. Filer didn't know if Buddha had a limit, but he had a fifty dollar limit and after he spent the fifty dollars he left for his trailer and a good night's sleep.

Chapter 58

At the trailer Girlfriend stretched in a lazy way with paws forward in a down dog yoga posture; then she recovered and came to rub against Filer's ankles.

"It's dinner time huh Kitty. Okay, okay I'll get on it."

Filer opened a can of cat food and put it in her bowl.

After dinner Girlfriend curled up on the sofa and settled in for an extended cat nap.

"This is good," Filer thought as he showered and got ready for bed. "I'll get a good night's sleep without the bed hog."

At midnight Filer was woken up by the same kind of crying like moan he'd heard before. It wasn't Girlfriend snoring and he didn't think a coyote could make that kind of sound. Also it sounded close like in his neighbor's trailer. Whatever the couple next door was up to he didn't like the sound of it. Filer had just gotten back to sleep when he felt Girlfriend snuggle into her favorite place beside him. It looked like he was going to have to put up with the Siamese for the rest of the night.

Next morning, at six o'clock, Filer was up and having breakfast. He wasn't entirely convinced the trip with Buddha was a good idea, but it was probably better than sitting around all day in the trailer.

Chapter 59

Shortly after he finished eating and putting the dishes in the sink Filer heard the gravel outside the trailer crunching under truck tires.

"That must be Buddha," he said to Kitty. He had already let Kitty out for a run and a roll in the dirt so she was good to be indoors with the litter box.

Buddha knocked on the door.

"Hey Buddha, what's up?" Filer greeted Buddha with a smile. He stepped out of the trailer and got into the passenger side of Buddha's pickup.

"Mr. Mad Dog, we're going to a ghost town called Unionville. Samuel, the prospector, has a hermit's shack just outside the town."

"Does Samuel make any money prospecting?" Filer asked.

"Depends on what you call money? He doesn't make the kind of money we make, but he makes enough money to live off the grid. You know a subsistence kind of living. Actually I haven't seen anyone as suited to the Nevada desert as Samuel. He knows how to live off the land.

If he gets desperate he hunts rattlesnakes. He says he doesn't like hunting the snakes but he does it if funds get a little short."

"Who buys the rattlesnakes?"

"A University buys some for research, and a company that makes antidotes for snake bites buys some. He doesn't hunt snakes very often; only when the University or the antidote company asks for them."

"Samuel sounds like a real interesting man."

"Samuel's day job, if you want to call it that is what you're interested in. He works the abandoned mines for grocery money."

Filer asked again, "Does he make any money?"

"He does good enough to support himself in the desert. Samuel says he makes all he needs because he doesn't need what most people need."

"I can hardly wait to meet him," Filer said.

"You'll be surprised," Buddha replied.

Buddha kept his eyes on the road and the two men sat in silence for the next twenty minutes. Then they passed through a ghost town. Filer noticed the faded buildings and falling down store fronts.

"Looks like nobody's home," Filer joked.

Buddha nodded at Filer's comment. "Unionville had its time in the 1880's and 90's. They were digging gold out of the mine here by the ton. I'm not talking about the kind of gold we mine, but main veins of gold bright enough to be seen right in front of your eyes. But like ghost towns all over the territory the mine played out and that was all that was keeping the population in the boom towns. Once the gold was gone the saloons and whore houses disappeared. The churches and general stores didn't last much longer. People were off to the next hot strike or somewhere to farm or work nine to five jobs where ever they could find them.

There just aren't enough natural resources other than gold and silver to support people out here in the desert."

"I grew up in Idaho," Filer said. "Idaho has its ghost towns and near ghost towns with a few shops open to tourists. Idaho City is surrounded by piles of tailings left behind by dredges. That was back before gold mining outfits had to do reclaim like today. They left enough mercury in the streams so it supposedly still isn't safe to eat fish caught in the mountain creeks and streams."

Filer thought for a minute and then continued. "But when there is a lot of irrigation in farming communities it probably isn't too good of an idea to eat fish that survive in the pesticide run off from the farm fields."

"It's a hell've world now-a-days," Buddha agreed. "There are too many people to feed without the help of modern science. And we're in too much of a hurry to feed people safely."

Just out of Unionville Buddha took a left off of 400 heading into the desert. All Filer could see was sagebrush and Juniper trees, a common landscape in this part of Nevada. The ground was covered in dull brown grasses. During the next five minutes they drove through grassy sand dunes and finally found a shack with a metal roof.

As far as Filer could tell the shack looked like any abandoned desert dwelling. Beside the shack there was a thirty year old pickup. The rusted pickup matched its desert surroundings.

Buddha led the way to the shack door. He knocked but there was no answer.

"You sure Samuel knew we were coming?" Filer asked.

"Nope, I just took a chance we'd find him here. He never gets very far from his shack."

Buddha knocked again with no answer again.

"I don't know," Filer thought, "we might have come a long way on a wild goose chase."

Chapter 60

A rustling noise came from the side of the shack. The source of the noise came around the front corner of the desert dwelling. A full grown wolf stared at the two men standing at the front door. Before they could react further a bearded man wearing a Hawaiian shirt, khaki shorts and a long billed cap with a back flap appeared behind the wolf.

"Buddha," the man greeted them.

Buddha handed Sam a six pack of Coors.

"Sam, I see Wolfy is still putting up with you."

The wolf wagged its tail and came to Buddha looking to get a chin scratch.

Filer relaxed when the wolf sat on its haunches like a regular pet; and he turned his attention to the animal's owner.

Samuel Lewis lived alone after half a lifetime of observing and distrusting his fellow human beings. Despite living solo he maintained a respect for the small number of people he depended on as friends. Samuel wasn't a psychopath or a sociopath, he just preferred his own company to that of most people.

To survive in his solitary life Samuel learned to live off of what nature could provide for him.

Summers were Samuel's busy time. He trapped rattlesnakes to sell to herpetologist who milked them for their venom. He also mined lost mines for the few ounces of gold it took to stock his pantry for the winter months. To protect his livelihood Samuel added secrecy to his slightly anti-social personality.

Buddha met Samuel at an all you can eat buffet in Winnemucca. Two drunks with low I.Q.'s were hassling Samuel. They saw Samuel selling gold dust in a pawn shop and followed him to the buffet. They sat on either side of Samuel and were threatening him. Buddha played peace keeper.

Chapter 61

"Gentleman, I think you are not wanted here," Buddha mediated.

Samuel looked up at Buddha.

"Everyone here is behaving in a civilized way and you two are causing a disturbance."

"Why don't you just bud out pecker head," the first drunk said.

"I tell you what; if this gentleman tells me to bud out I'll leave. If he doesn't say anything you two will leave."

"If we don't leave, then what?"

"I'm a peaceful man, but I'll guess we'll just have to see."

The two drunks stood up and confronted Buddha.

"You don't want to do this," Buddha cautioned them.

"We'll see, you nosy bastard," the talkative thug said and he took a swing at Buddha.

Buddha pushed his fist aside and hit him with a strategic blow in the throat that knocked him to his knees. The second thug stared open mouthed at Buddha just long enough for Buddha to kick him in the knee and slam his fist into the side of his head under his ear. The thug went down landing on top of the first man.

By this time casino security caught up with the action and arrested both of the drunks and held them for the police.

Samuel smiled at Buddha, "I owe you a drink."

From that time on Samuel and Buddha were good friends. Buddha visited Samuel in his desert camp a couple of time a month.

Chapter 62

"Sam, this is my friend Filer. He just started with Pegasus and he hasn't seen any gold yet. I thought I'd bring him out to your place so he could get a look at the real thing."

"Well come in and I'll see what I can find."

Filer followed Buddha into what he thought would be a broken down desert lean-to. Instead he saw a comfortable living space next to a small but efficient kitchen. Wolfy took his place on a padded dog bed.

Buddha spoke, "Sam isn't your typical prospector. Ask anyone and they'll tell you he has a nose for gold. The real mystery is why he doesn't use his nose to live a little less like a hermit."

Sam went to the refrigerator and produced three beers. He handed his visitors each a cold beer and then took a seat in his easy chair.

"If I was living like a real hermit I wouldn't have guys like you coming out here drinking my beers and bothering Wolfy," Sam said and smiled. Filer looked at the wolf with its chin resting dog like on its front paws.

"Come on Sam, you're Sam the Nugget Man," Buddha said.

"That CB handle was a big mistake. I'd take it back if I could."

"Your secret fortress is safe with me," Buddha reassured Sam.

"You're one of the few who knows where I'm living now. It got so bad I had two or three people per month coming out to see me. That's two too many for me and Wolfy. What do you think Filer?" Sam smiled at Filer.

"I'm a family man," Filer said. "But when I'm working I'm like a hermit without my family with me. You know how it is; the wife wants a home next to a good school, a supermarket and a decent mall."

"How do you feel living alone?" Sam asked.

"I'd rather have my family with me, but I know some guys who are away from home for a week and have a girlfriend keeping them company before the week is up.

How about you Sam?"

"I've got Wolfy during the day time and the U.F.O.'s at night."

Before Filer could question the U.F.O. comment, Sam asked him, "What about you?"

"I've got a girlfriend, but I wouldn't want her anywhere near Wolfy."

"Why's that?"

"Girlfriend is a Siamese cat that adopted me in a trailer park in Montana on my last job away from home; and I think she would give Wolfy a run for his money if he got her riled up."

Samuel got back on the subject. "So you're a faithful family man."

"I look but I don't touch."

Buddha interrupted to get their visit back on track, "What about it Sam? Do you have any nuggets Filer can take a look at? Who can you trust if you don't trust a faithful family man?"

"Yeah, I've got a couple of nuggets tucked away."

Sam went to the cupboards over the kitchen stove. He reached inside the cupboard and pulled out a coffee can.

Filer didn't know if it was good idea to keep gold in a coffee can. He'd checked the price of gold when Cochrane had offered him the job and it was now 328 dollars an ounce.

Sam sat down at the table and pulled the lid off of the can. He spilled nuggets onto the table top between the beers.

Again Filer thought, "I hope this man doesn't show the nuggets to everyone who comes around."

Sam noticed the concerned look on Filer's face and he smiled. "I don't get that many visitors out here and I trust Buddha like family. Hell, I trust him better than family; and I have Wolfy and the Defender." Sam said and pointed at a 2x4 with a carved handle by the door.

Buddha smiled proudly and glanced at Filer.

"Go ahead and pick 'em up," Sam told Filer.

Filer picked up the two largest nuggets and weighed them in his palm.

Sam looked at him questioningly.

"They're heavy," Filer said with a smile.

"I found those in an abandoned mine. I followed a vein that looked played out and dug a little deeper."

"Don't get me wrong. I was really lucky to find nuggets that large. That doesn't happen that often. You find a lot of dust before you find nuggets."

"Pegasus is mining to find dust," Buddha said.

"You're right," Sam added. "And that's why I can still make a little money prospecting these old claims. The early mining companies found what gold they could find with the technology of their time and then they moved on. They shut down and left a lot of ghost towns like Unionville behind."

Filer asked, "Do you make enough to live on?"

Well, first of all, I don't need a lot. If you've got time to look at my set up I'll explain why."

"What I'm really proud of is my solar and wind power set-ups. That's what makes it a lot easier to stay off the grid."

"I have a windmill that raises water from a hundred foot well. Most of the time I don't have to make water runs. Usually the lack of water discourages a lot of us hermits."

Filer and Buddha sat waiting for more.

Sam lifted a cloth hanging over the edge of a table in the kitchen and showed them several batteries hooked together. "I have a solar cell following the sun that charges these batteries. A converter changes the electricity in the batteries to 110 volts for use in the shack. I could run a TV or a washing machine if I wanted to, but I don't need either of them. I have a CB radio, a small fridge, and the electric lighting; they're all I need to keep me happy."

From his experience as a lineman Filer had seen solar setups before. He hadn't made his mind up as to the usefulness of solar energy to replace electrical systems as he knew them.

Filer smiled, "I've worked on a lot of powerlines in the Northwest and solar power might be okay for a few isolated shacks here and there, but I don't think it'll be able to replace the national power grids."

"You're right Filer. I won't argue the point. But for a few of us hermit types it works out just fine."

Filer smiled and nodded at Sam.

"Tell him about the rattlesnakes," Buddha said.

"It doesn't take much talent to catch a rattlesnake or two to sell to the University. You can go out with me sometime when I go hunting."

"All I have to do is find a few handfuls of gold and a few rattlesnakes to keep me going." Sam smiled at his guests and hand them both new cold beers.

"With Wolfy here I'm not alone and he's about as good of company as most humans I know-present company excepted of course," Sam said.

Buddha said, "No need for exceptions; I'm sure Filer understands animal company very well."

All three men sipped their beers in silence for a couple of minutes and Wolfy came to sit by Sam's chair.

When the beers were finished Buddha thanked Sam for his hospitality and invited him to Winnemucca whenever he wanted to visit. Sam shook hands with Filer and invited him out anytime.

"Thanks," Filer said, and added, "You can call me Mad Dog."

"Well, Mad Dog the invitation still stands."

On the drive back to Winnemucca Buddha told Filer Sam had had a life at one time, a wife and a daughter, but they died in a car crash. After the crash Sam moved to the desert.

Chapter 63

Back at his trailer Filer waved as Buddha drove away, then he went inside and Girlfriend wrapped herself around his ankles.

"What is it Girlfriend? You want something to eat?

Filer went to the kitchen and opened a can of cat food. While Girlfriend ate he settled into his easy chair to watch TV. The reception was bad so he adjusted the rabbit ear antenna until he got a program. The program was *American Daddy* and there she was-Kylie. She didn't look like the little girl who used to help him build model houses. She was dressed like the other women on the show. He felt disappointed that there wasn't anything he could do to help the adopted daughter he'd brought to California.

The ten o'clock news came on and Filer watched until he nodded off. A little later he woke up when he heard the coyote howling. But the howl sounded like a long drawn out no-o-o. "Just my imagination," Filer thought. He turned the TV off and went to bed.

Chapter 64

During the next two weeks Filer got to know the reclaim crews. He had been with them after work and went to a barbeque with Chuy on the weekend. The routine of a heavy equipment operator came back to him.

On a Friday morning of the third week Cochrane left a note for the reclaim foreman to bring Filer into the manager's office.

"What docs Cochrane want me for?" Filer asked.

"I don't know," Bill answered.

Bill dropped Filer off at the main building.

"Good luck, Mad Dog," Bill said.

Filer didn't know what to think. Bill hadn't said anything. "He's a pretty good foreman," Filer thought. "He would have said something if he knew something. But Bill had never used his nick name before." Just that made Filer nervous as he walked to Cochrane's office.

Denise smiled at Filer and told him to wait a minute while she called Cochrane over the intercom.

"Mr. Cochrane, Filer Wilson is here," she said holding the intercom button down.

Cochrane's voice sounded out of the machine. "Send him in."

Denise smiled again and pointed at the door to Cochrane's office.

Filer entered Cochrane's office still not knowing what to expect. Inside the office he saw an attractive middle-aged woman sitting in one of the two chairs in front of Cochrane's desk.

"Take a seat," Cochrane told Filer.

Filer did as he was told.

"Filer, I've been hearing good things about you from Bill and the reclaim crew."

"Nice to know," Filer thought.

"Bill says you've filled in as a loader operator a couple of times."

"I've done that," Filer agreed.

"That's what we need on our main crew. I'll keep that in mind at the end of the reclaim."

Again Filer thought, "Okay."

"Listen Filer I've got a small situation on my hands."

"Here it comes," Filer thought.

"This is Wendy Jones. I guess I should say Dr. Jones. She's an archaeologist hired by Pegasus to make sure we explore our mining sites by the book," Cochrane paused.

Filer glanced at the woman.

"My problem is I need a Bobcat driver at Dr. Jones site. She's found Native American remains at her site and needs professional help digging a little deeper."

Cochrane studied Filer as if he could see Filer thinking. "Don't let this be happening to me."

"You'll be working for Dr. Jones for the next week. A Bobcat has already been delivered to her dig site. No need for you to come to the show up every morning. Dr. Jones will fill out your time card."

"Well I guess that's it Mr. Wilson. Look at this assignment as a learning experience. I'll want to know whatever you learn during your assignment. Today you can follow Dr. Jones to her site. Denise will issue you a gas credit card."

Filer stood up and left Cochrane's office. When he entered the reception area Denise had a gas card ready.

"Sign here Mr. Wilson," Denise said and smiled.

Since he really didn't know Denise he had to assume her smile indicated she knew he was going to be working for the woman he was leaving with. He didn't know her enough to do any back and forth with her so all he could do was say, "Thanks."

Chapter 65

Dr. Jones exited the Pegasus Company building and walked with Filer to his pickup.

"Mr. Wilson..." Filer interrupted the woman. He figured he'd put her on the right road from the beginning. "Call me Mad Dog."

"Okay," Wendy smiled. "Mad Dog, Mr. Cochrane said you should follow me to our dig site."

Filer nodded his agreement.

Dr. Jones walked to her Ford pickup. She left double skid marks when she gunned her truck out of the gravel parking lot.

"At least she's not afraid to drive her vehicle," Filer thought.

They kept to gravel backroads belonging to Pegasus and traveled twenty miles to a remote desert site. The site reminded Filer of sites he'd been to all of his working life. He saw the Bobcat loader/scraper parked by a marked off half acre site.

The sky shone brightly with a few clouds hanging over the desert. Dr. Jones reached into her pickup bed and grabbed a satchel. She waited by the truck for Filer to come to her.

Filer walked to Dr. Jones' pickup and stood beside her while she looked in her satchel. She pulled out some sheets with pictures on them.

"I doubt you'll spot anything from the Bobcat, but these are a few of the items we might find."

Filer saw pictures of small arrow heads and larger spear points. The sheets also illustrated grinding stones and grinding platforms.

"You could also see bones, doubtful yet possible. If you do see anything that looks interesting no matter what it might be stop and one of our team will come and take a look.

Try to take away the soil in thin layers, the thinner the better. We have the site marked with stakes. Once you get down to the marked level stop and we'll come and look for artifacts. When we have covered the excavated area you can go down another layer. Do you have any questions Mr. Wilson?"

Filer had listened closely while Dr. Jones explained; then he said, "We'll get along better if you call me Mad Dog like we agreed. That's my work name."

A bearded man joined them. He wore a plaid shirt and blue jeans.

Dr. Jones looked slightly annoyed, "Okay Mad Dog, you can call me Dr. Jones that's my work name. I'm going to leave one of my team here for an extra pair of eyes while you're excavating. Ed is one of my staff and an Assistant Professor."

The bearded man held out his hand and introduced himself. "My name's Ed. Ed's my work name when I'm not in the classroom," Ed said and smiled at Filer.

Dr. Jones spoke to Ed out of range for Filer to hear and then walked back to her pickup.

Ed got serious, "This is a sensitive area; if I see something I want to take a closer look at I'll give you a hand signal to stop scrapping."

Filer nodded that he understood what he was supposed to do.

Filer hadn't operated a Bobcat before. Cochrane hadn't asked if he had experience on one, so Filer assumed it was a learn as you go assignment. He'd be here on his own so he could go slow and get onto the Bobcat's operation as he went along. He started the Bobcat and experimented with the blade controls. Ed was watching from the sidelines at Filer moved the Bobcat into position and began to push dirt toward the edges of the area to be cleared.

From the sidelines Ed perked up and moved close to the area being scrapped. The desert soil accumulated at the borders around the site. Along with the soil prairie grasses and rocks were pushed to the edges.

After the first level of soil was removed Filer stopped the Bobcat and got down to talk to Ed.

Filer walked to stand beside Ed. "What do you think so far?"

"Didn't really expect to find much on top," Ed explained. "I watched but I didn't see anything of interest."

"How deep do you need to go?" Filer asked.

"This is a sensitive site. So we're going down a couple of feet."

"Do you want to keep taking it down inches at a time," Filer asked.

"Well, let's keep it at inches for the next couple of runs."

"You're the boss," Filer said.

Filer got back on the Bobcat and started scrapping soil again.

The two men continued working together. Filer ran the Bobcat and Ed kept his eyes on the ground being exposed. At twelve o'clock Wendy drove up and Ed signaled for Filer to shut the Bobcat down.

"What's up?" Filer asked.

"It's time for lunch," Ed replied. "We're going to base for lunch."

Both men climbed into Wendy's pickup and she drove them a mile on the gravel road to where Filer could see tents set up around a central cleared area.

Up close Filer noticed Ed was wearing an arrowhead necklace.

"What do you think of our dig Mad Dog?" Wendy asked.

Filer smiled a little, "Real exciting," Filer said.

Ed smiled when he heard Filer's reply.

"It'll get better," Ed said and glanced at Wendy. "I'll show you some nice artifacts we've found."

Filer could tell they were both enthusiastic about their work. The job wasn't just a nine to five job for them.

"First of all we'll feed you a good lunch," Wendy promised.

Chapter 66

The archaeology team sat on wooden benches at folding tables. A student assistant stood at a Weber grill turning hamburgers and hotdogs. A table nearby was filled with buns, potato salad, potato chips, a fresh vegetable tray and a variety of garnishes for the burgers and dogs. A wash tub filled with ice, beers, and soda sat at one end of the table.

Filer observed the people around him. They were just boys and girls, not much older than Kylie. Dr. Jones and Ed were the exceptions. Dr. Jones was probably older than Filer, and Ed was just his age. They were the parent figures of the group.

"What do you want Mad Dog, a burger or a dog?" Ed asked.

"I'll take a burger," Filer replied.

"Okay," Ed said and handed him a paper plate with a burger on it.

If he was back at his regular job Filer would be eating a lunch he'd made out of out of a lunch box. It wouldn't be a picnic like this.

"You're running the Bobcat aren't you?" a young blonde asked Filer.

"Yeah, I got pulled off of a D10 dozer to help out here."

"What do you think of our dig so far?"

"Looks like prairie grass, dirt and sand pushed off of the desert."

"Wait until you uncover an artifact. You don't know what it's like until you get connected to history."

Filer had had many of these types of conversations. This student was really into primitive Native American cultures and the items they left behind. Sports freaks know the life time batting averages, basketball stats, and football goals of their favorite players. Hunters and fishermen had their personal tall tales to tell.

Filer knew the machines he ran and the ones he had to operate around. He knew how to deal with bosses and foremen, and he had a tall tale or two of his own to tell about his years as a lineman.

Now sitting here with the blonde he could look interested and he might even remember a little of what fascinated her but he seldom got the look in his eyes as she had while she explained the difference between Clovis and Solutrean spear points. Whatever the difference whoever made the spear points were long gone, not just generations but hundreds of years in the past.

Filer thought Abbey and Kylie talked about the Hollywood scene the way these students talked about the dig. They got all excited about stars they got a peek at in restaurants or at Shane's place.

"Hey," the blonde said, "Are you okay? You look kind of spaced out."

"Yeah, I'm good. I was just thinking of my daughter. She's your age and she's on this TV show called *American Daddy*. Have you seen it?"

"I don't watch much TV, especially when we're out here." But the blonde stopped, looked surprised, and then said, "I have seen the show."

"What do you think of it?"

"To be honest, I think it's one of the sleaziest shows on TV. The way they treat women is the worst."

"My friend in Hollywood told me the same thing." Filer paused, "My daughter's boyfriend is one of the stars. He's the one who got her a place on the show. I don't like him or the show. My daughter is an adult and I can't tell her what to do. When she was younger I would run a loser like the one she's with now off."

"How did your daughter meet the loser?" Filer felt a little uncomfortable explaining the story about how he came to be in Hollywood. Yet after he'd told the story several times he was starting to realize there was something to Rupert's novel and movie.

"A friend of mine wrote a story partly about my time as a lineman in Farewell Bend, Oregon."

At this point the only way to complete the explanation was to tell the whole tale of the murder, his electrocution, and his marriage to Abbey and the adoption of Kylie.

By the time Filer finished telling his story several of the students were listening to him.

"That's how Kylie got a part on *American Daddy* because she was in Hollywood with me and Abbey while I advised the director of *Copper Thieves.*"

"Wow, you're like a celebrity," the blonde smiled.

"No I'm a lineman who gave up line work to be a dozer operator. *Copper Thieves,* the movie, is finished and I would like Abbey and Kylie here with me. She got the part on *American Daddy* so Abbey is staying with her in Hollywood. If anyone is a celebrity it's Kylie."

Dr. Jones came out of her tent and announced, "Okay everyone lunch is over. Let's get back to work."

"I see you've got some admirers," Dr. Jones said.

The lineman's law of tall tales took over. "There's a book out with me in it," Filer began. "And now there'll be a movie with Mad Dog as one of the characters. If you want a book I can get one for you."

"Well I guess I'd better get a book," Wendy said. "How much?"

"For friends there's no charge."

I've written a book," Wendy said. "How are you making any money giving books away?"

"Don't worry. They're promotion copies. Tell your friends if the book is a good read, and get them to buy a copy. Actually if you want to know about line work you should read *Mad Dog Steel Time. Steel Time* is about a job I did building steel transmission towers in Montana. It's a little more straight forward than *Copper Thieves.* There is a lot of fiction mixed up in the story but no murders."

Wendy said, "My book is all facts and figures with some pictures of people and artifacts. It appeals to students and teachers who are interested in the same things I'm interested in. Oh there may be a few civilians who want to read it. If you want to get ahead in archaeology you have to publish. It's called publish or perish."

"Sounds kind of harsh," Filer sympathized.

"Well it's what I signed up for and I enjoy working and teaching archaeology. This dig could be very important if we come up with the right artifacts."

Chapter 67

Dr. Jones, Ed, and Filer rode back to the dig site in Dr. Jones' pickup. Dr. Jones stopped her truck and walked to the dig with Filer and Ed. She inspected the site where soil had been scrapped away.

Filer stopped beside Wendy before he started the Bobcat up.

"It doesn't look like anything so far," Wendy said. "But we're hoping to start finding artifacts at the one foot level. Keep scrapping and Ed will keep an eye on the site as you work it."

Filer started the Bobcat and started pushing dirt. As a machine the Bobcat, compared to a D10, was a little tipsy. It had taken a while and now he was getting used to the delicate nature of the Bobcat. Now he could pay more attention to the surface of the dig as he uncovered it; and he didn't need to worry because Ed was keeping watch from the side of the dig.

The sky shone bright blue in a cloudless setting. The day couldn't be better for working outdoors. Filer had worked his share of crappy days as a lineman. Winter work was the worst. Handling tools with cold stiff hands and stomping feet to keep from freezing. There had been good days like this one, but he had still been hiking poles and taking his life into his own hands to do everyday business.

Filer parked the Bobcat at five-thirty. His first day working with the archaeologist had been an easy day. They hadn't found anything besides empty pop bottles and rusty beer cans. It was the kind of trash that turned up everywhere.

Chapter 68

It was good to get back to the trailer. There weren't any messages, but Girlfriend was definitely happy to see him. Anyway, she was as happy as he supposed cats ever got to see humans. Filer freshened Girlfriend's water, and opened a can of cat food for her. As soon as the cat food hit the bowl Girlfriend forgot all about Filer.

After cleaning up Filer watched a TV show called *Explaining UFO's*. He hadn't made up his mind about them yet. Filer wasn't religious. He liked how Buddha talked about Buddhism and Buddha not being a God in his lifetime. And then his followers made him into a God after he died and his teachings into a religion.

In his mind UFO's might be part of the bigger picture. UFO's could have something to do with the Gods as early man saw them. They would be so far outside man's experience that the only way mankind could think of them was to make them into Gods. Filer called Buddha and asked him for Sam's CB handle. Sam said, "He got to you didn't he?"

"What do you mean?"

"Sam's like that. He could start a cult if he wanted to. But Sam's a good man and he doesn't take advantage of people."

"Well that's not exactly what I was thinking. He said he's seen UFO's and I want to ask him if he'd show them to me."

"Okay Mad Dog. Sorry I got carried away."

After finishing the call to Buddha Filer got in his pickup and called Sam on his CB radio. "Hi Nugget Man, it's Mad Dog-Buddha's friend."

"Yeah sure, I remember. You wanted to see some real gold."

Filer thought it was Buddha who wanted to show him some real gold, but he let it go.

"I'd like to see a UFO. You said you've seen UFO's."

"Well Mad Dog they don't keep a regular schedule, but we can do a stakeout like cops do. We go to a place where I've seen them before and spend some time watching for them."

"How long do you think it will take?"

Sam laughed. "It's not like that. We'd have to take a chance."

Filer thought for a minute, "When can I come out?"

"Why don't you come out tomorrow after dinner?"

"Thanks," Filer said.

Later, when he got comfortably situated in bed Girlfriend came into the bedroom and jumped onto the middle of the bed so that Filer had to make room for her. He couldn't figure out how an animal so small could be such a nuisance. He figured it was a nuisance he could put up with. As he told people she had saved his sanity many times. That was more than he could say for most people he knew.

Chapter 69

The next morning Filer retraced the route he and Buddha took to Sam's place. This time he thought he noticed an old pickup behind him. He wasn't really concentrating on anything except the road ahead, besides the western states were filled with pickups of every description.

He pulled into a service station to get a fill-up and the truck he thought he'd seen sped by down the road.

After the fill-up Filer felt better about the old pickup and got back on the road not worrying that he was being followed.

Normally Filer wasn't the paranoid or conspiracy type so it had bothered him thinking he had seen a guy following him the past couple of weeks.

Further ahead the old pickup was waiting for Filer to go by. Filer didn't notice the vehicle pull back on the road and continue following him.

A short distance later Filer left the paved road for the desert trail to Sam's desert shack. The vehicle following him stayed behind the dust being kicked up by Filer's truck. It was the hitman Steve Williams had hired from prison.

Chapter 70

At Sam's shack Filer parked his pickup and knocked on Sam's door.

"Hi there, Mad Dog. How are you doing?" Wolfy stuck his head out the door.

"I'm doing okay Sam. How are you?"

"Same as always, Mad Dog. Just got back from a snake hunt and I've got a couple of rattlers to milk in the hamper over there."

"What about the UFO's?"

"We'll we have to wait a little after sunset. They're easier to see after dark. Come in and we'll have a couple of beers while we wait. Do you want to take another look at the nuggets?"

"No I just came for the U.F.O.'s," Filer said.

While Filer and Sam waited for sunset the hitman was sneaking up on them. He slipped past the parked vehicles and up to the shack. Being very careful he peaked through a window and saw Filer and Sam relaxing with beers. He got interested when he heard Sam mention gold nuggets.

Wolfy was asleep on his dog bed, and then he was awake and growling.

"What's wrong Wolfy?" Sam said.

Just after Wolfy growled a loud bang came from the door. Before either Sam or Filer could get to their feet the door crashed open and a tattooed man stepped through the ruined door.

"What the hell?" Filer said. He saw the man pointing a gun at him.

Wolfy growled again and ran past Sam to jump at the gun man. The gun man fired a shot. At that range he couldn't miss and Wolfy fell to the floor of the shack.

"You shouldn't have done that," Sam informed the assassin.

"Shut-up or you'll be on the floor with the mutt."

"Wolfy isn't a mutt. He's one hundred percent wolf," Sam said. "Whatever. Listen up old man. I want your gold. I know you've got nuggets here."

Filer looked at Sam and nodded toward the hamper with the rattlesnake in it.

"No," Sam said, and then he caught on to Filer's idea.

"Okay, you get the gold and then you get the hell out of here so I can take care of Wolfy."

"That's real nice old man. Where's the nuggets?"

Sam was kneeling over Wolfy. Filer was still in his chair.

"It's in the clothes hamper over in the corner under the laundry bag."

Filer watched the gun man back up to the plastic clothes hamper keeping his attention on Sam until he got to the hamper.

With the gun pointed at Filer and Sam the tattooed man fumbled with the hamper lid and stuck his hand into the hamper. Once his hand was in the hamper he glanced down and saw a six foot diamond back desert rattler sink two inch fangs into his arm and inject deadly venom.

The gun man howled with surprise and pain and stumbled backwards with the rattler still attached to his arm. He tried pointing the gun at the snake and in pain he pulled the trigger. He hit the snake and his arm.

Filer picked up the two by four Sam kept by the door and slammed it beside the gun man's head. He went down, falling on top of the snake. He was out cold.

Sam got his snake wrangling pole and captured the angry snake. He put the rattler back in the hamper and replaced the lid.

"What do you think Filer?"

"Well we better get Wolfy to the vet." Filer smiled, "And maybe the vet can do something for the bad guy."

Sam also smiled. "It's better than he deserves," Sam replied.

The two men tied the tattooed man up so that the ropes also acted like a tourniquet.

Sam called the vet on his CB radio and told him they would be coming in with a gunshot Wolfy, and they would also have a snake bite victim. "Call the sheriff and maybe have an ambulance there."

"What?"

"I'll explain when we get there."

"I'll organize it," the vet replied.

Filer and Sam put Wolfy in the front seat of Filer's pickup and threw the bad guy in the pickup bed.

Chapter 71

As soon as Filer and Sam arrived at Dr. Clay Handler's veterinarian clinic Dr. Handler turned the hitman over to an ambulance crew and the sheriff. Then he took Wolfy into his operating room. The unconscious wolf panted weakly as the vet placed him on his operating table.

The vet probed the wound and extracted a bullet from the wolf's shoulder. He cleaned and bandaged the wound, and then with Sam's help he placed Wolfy in a kennel on a padded bed.

Dr. Handler had been giving Wolfy his shots and general health care since he was a pup. The vet was a good man and he cared as much for the wolf as Sam did.

"Well Sam unless something unexpected happens, Wolfy should be as good as new in a couple of weeks. Leave him here with me for a couple of days so I can keep an eye on him."

"Alright Clay, I'll come back with a nugget or two in three days."

The ambulance crew took the handcuffed hitman to the hospital. After being treated for snakebite and the self-inflicted gunshot wound he ended up in the city jail.

The sheriff took Sam's and Filer's statements and charged the hitman with armed robbery and assault. The charge would later be changed to attempted murder for hire.

It was after dark when Filer and Sam got into Filer's pickup for the trip back to Sam's shack.

"That was good thinking with the snake," Sam said.

"It could have gone wrong. He didn't have to put his hand in the hamper."

Chapter 72

Sam was quiet until they got to the turn off to his shack.

"Take a right here Mad Dog," Sam motioned to a trail leading into tall sagebrush and Juniper bushes.

"Where are we going Sam?"

"It's just about the right time to see some UFO's," Sam replied.

Filer took the turn-off into the sagebrush filled desert.

"Stop here," Sam said and added, "Too bad we didn't bring any binoculars. Anyway this is the best place to see the UFO's."

Same got out of the pickup and went into the sagebrush. When he got back Filer gave him a questioning look.

"Had to take a pee," Sam explained.

Filer nodded.

"Now we wait," Sam said.

Both men leaned against the pickup scanning the night sky.

"There," Sam said and pointed at a place in the sky.

"What should I be looking for?" Filer asked.

"Watch there," Sam said and pointed again.

Filer looked where Sam was pointing and finally saw red points of light darting across the sky.

"You see," Sam said, "Shooting stars don't go back and forth like that. They only go one way."

"I don't know," Filer said.

"Think about it," Sam said, "What else could they be? They aren't satellites. Satellites stay in orbit without jumping back and forth."

"What about airplanes?" Filer suggested.

"Airplanes don't go that high," Sam said.

"Okay," Filer said, "We're looking at UFO's. Do they ever come any closer?"

"Not so far," Sam said.

After watching in wonder for a couple more minutes Filer and Sam got back in the pickup and Filer drove Sam back to his desert home.

"Thanks for that Sam," Filer said.

"It's the least I could do," Sam said.

On the way back to Winnemucca Filer wondered what to do with his new information about UFO's. Would anyone believe him without seeing what he saw?

As he went into his trailer he decided it was too late to think about UFO's

Girlfriend was fast asleep on the couch and for once stayed asleep.

It had been a big day with a hitman, rattlesnakes, and UFO's. Too bad he couldn't talk about it with Abbey. Filer went to bed and fell asleep.

Chapter 73

Kylie watched Jeffery from off stage on set. He was in the middle of a dialogue with the father character. During this scene they were setting up for her scene. She had come to dread scenes where she had to deal with the father. He took every opportunity to put hands on her anywhere possible. The director never did anything to stop the actor no matter how bad he groped her. In fact he seemed to take pleasure in Kylie being uncomfortable during those moments.

Her boyfriend, she didn't know why she still considered him her boyfriend, also didn't say anything to the actor or the director about her treatment on the set. Kylie supposed she put up with her disgust on the set because she was now a part of *American Daddy* and an actor in Hollywood.

She knew Abbey saw what was going on during shooting. Abbey asked her what she wanted to do. Did she want to quit? Did she want to complain? She was leaving all of this up to Kylie. Kyle thought, "Why shouldn't she leave it up to me? I'm an adult, not a kid anymore."

In Nevada Filer didn't know what his adopted daughter was going through. Abbey had decided to keep her worries about Kylie to herself. And Kylie was stubborn enough to suffer in silence.

If Abbey and Kylie decided to tell Filer about the kind of abuse Kylie was putting up with her Hollywood career could be at an end after Filer confronted the people involved.

During her scene, Larry put his hand on her thigh while they were setting on the couch. Kylie put one hand on his wrist while she smiled at him and with the other hand she grabbed his middle finger and bent it backwards still smiling at him.

Larry got a surprised and painful look on his face and pulled his hand back.

Kylie leaned in close and whispered, "There's more where that came from if you want it."

Larry barely kept his cool and smiled at the camera and the puzzled director.

Kylie finished her scene with Larry keeping his hands to himself.

"Thanks Dyna," Kylie thought.

Chapter 74

At the end of his first week at the dig site Filer had lowered half a football field approximately one foot. He and Ed had become friends. Ed might be an Assistant Professor but he enjoyed a beer or two after work and he liked to play the slots. Ed was divorced and he enjoyed talking about being able to play the field again.

"You know Mad Dog Co-eds aren't what they used to be. They read Cosmo and Betty Freidan. It seems like all they want now-a-days is an education."

Filer smiled. He had dated before he married Abbey and it had been easy to come into a small town as part of a hard partying line crew and pick up single party girls looking for a guy who would spend a little money on them at the local hot spot. This had suited him because he wasn't looking for a church girl.

He liked Abbey because she wasn't a church woman and she liked to have fun at the bars. On the other hand Abbey was a single mother when they first met. He moved into her spare bedroom. His kitchen privileges had evolved into boyfriend with benefits and when the job in Farewell Bend, Oregon ended he asked Abbey to marry him. Or had it been Abbey suggested it to him. Whichever, now they were a functioning couple. It only bothered him that they were a long distance couple. Abbey and Kylie in Hollywood was a development he couldn't have guessed would happen. He would be happy if all of it ended and they could go back to their old lives together.

Chapter 75

Back on the job, at the dig next day Filer saw Ed raise his hand.

"Hey Mad Dog hold on a minute," Ed yelled from his vantage point outside of the dig.

Filer took his foot off the accelerator and stopped the Bobcat.

"What do you have Ed?"

"Come and take a look."

Filer climbed off of the Bobcat and walked to Ed's side.

"Mad Dog do you know what coprolite is?"

"I don't know Ed," Filer answered smiling. He could tell when a joke was coming.

"It's fossilized shit, Filer. And we won't be leaving any of our shit behind to become fossilized," Ed explained.

Filer raised an eyebrow.

"Look over there," Ed pointed down the road.

Down the gravel road leading to the dig site a pickup truck pulling a flatbed with a green Porta-Potty on it came to a stop.

"Yep, Mad Dog, you have to hand it to OSHA, they really came through. Whatta you think?"

Filer said, "I've been pissing and shitting in the sagebrush for years, so thank you OSHA. Now I'll have a little comfort of home right out here in the desert."

"Well," Ed said, "You have to give them credit for protecting the environment."

Filer said, "I wonder if they'll get on our case if we piss on the ground?"

"We'd better be careful; they might have inspectors driving by at any time."

Both men laughed and Filer went back to the Bobcat.

Filer climbed back into the Bobcat and started it up. He looked over the Bobcat's blade and saw Ed enter the Porta-Potty. He stopped the Bobcat and waited for Ed to come out of the Porta-Potty. He had to laugh when he saw Ed open the door of the Porta-Potty and step out.

"It works," ED said and smiled.

For the next hour Filer worked the Bobcat taking the site down inch by inch. As he made an end turn and started back across the site he saw something that made him slow down. "Ed you'd better come look at this," Filer called to Ed.

Ed stepped onto the site and walked to stand beside Filer and the Bobcat.

Filer pointed at some rocks in the cleared area. "What do you think of that?" Filer asked.

"What?" Ed asked.

"There," Filer said nodding to the tops of a semi-circle of stones poking out of the ground.

"Holy shit," Ed said. "I think we've got something there."

Ed walked to the stones. "I think we've got a Fremont pit outline."

Filer looked like he needed more of an explanation.

"The Fremont peoples settled in Utah. We don't know much about them. It'll be a surprise to Dr. Jones. I'd better get her here right away."

"Huh," Filer shrugged his shoulders. "Ed what do you want me to do?"

"Come with me to the main camp. We'll get Wendy and a couple of the grad students to come out and take a look."

Chapter 76

Ed and Filer arrived at the main camp in Ed's pickup. Ed hurried to Dr. Jones' tent. When he got to the tent Filer was right behind him. Ed knocked on the tent post and then ducked inside.

Wendy looked up, "Ed, what's up? Did the Porta-Potty get there?"

"Yeah, yeah," Ed replied.

Before Ed could go on Wendy said, "Good. So what's your news?"

"You're not going to believe this Wendy. I think we've got the footprint of a Fremont pit house."

"You sure?"

"I'm not 100 percent sure. That's why you've got to come and see it."

Wendy looked at Filer over Ed's shoulder.

Filer wondered what it would be like to be involved in the dig like the archaeologists. They both looked very excited.

"Okay Ed. Let's go take a look and see what you've got. Do you know how exciting it would be if you really do have a pit house?"

"I sure do. It's right up there with finding the pot of gold at the end of the rainbow," Ed said.

"Mr. Wilson, e-e-r Mad Dog," Wendy said, "If this is a pit house you're going to be a lucky man. This is the kind of discovery grad students work years to be a part of."

Filer didn't register the kind of emotional response Ed and Wendy were expecting.

Chapter 77

Back at the area being cleared, Dr. Jones and Ed entered the cleared area by the barely exposed stone circle. They had hand scoops and brushes ready to uncover the stones.

Filer sat in the Bobcat. The two archaeologists were now ignoring him. He watched them carefully removing soil from the stone circle.

After forty-five minutes of sitting on the Bobcat the archaeologists took a break to sip coffee from Ed's thermos. It looked like they were going to continue ignoring Filer and then Dr. Jones spoke to him.

"Mad Dog it's too bad you're not an archaeologist. What you've helped us find is like having Christmas in July. We're uncovering a real discovery here,"

Wendy went on to describe what they'd found.

"This is the foundation of a Fremont pit house."

Filer walked to stand beside Wendy and Ed.

"You see the placement of the rocks. They were laid out in a circle and used as braces for lodge pole pines which were used as rafters. We've found pole holes where the poles rested against the stones."

Filer thought for a minute and then asked, "What were they doing out here in the middle of the desert?"

"Native Americans of this time period probably had several different homes or camps. They might have been following different mammal species during their migrations and the vegetation was different then. The Fremont peoples were hunter/gatherers. They moved to take advantage of the weather and the growing seasons.

Of course this is an anomaly because the Fremont traditionally occupied Utah. For them to be found here is a real discovery."

"Probably some lone guy trying to make a living for his family," Filer thought unconsciously comparing the situation to his modern day equivalent.

"We're going to take some pictures for *Archaeology Journal* and we want a shot of you on the Bobcat."

"I'll have to ask my foreman," Filer answered.

"We'll be here for a while," Dr. Jones said. "In the meantime we need to get another section of the site cleared of topsoil. We're hoping we have another pit house here. That would prove this wasn't an oddity."

"We're going back to camp now to organize the grad students to excavate the circle. Maybe after we get back you can help Ed measure out a new area to be cleared. And when we get to camp you can call your foreman and get permission to have your picture in the article."

At camp Filer used his CB radio to call Bill and get permission to be in a photograph of the site. Bill said he'd have to ask Cochrane if it was okay.

Bill called back and said, "Cochrane said its okay. It looks like you'll get your fifteen minutes of fame."

Filer didn't try to tell Bill he'd had all the fame he needed with his Hollywood adventure.

"Well I don't know about the fame part. I didn't do anything except operate the Bobcat."

"In my opinion they want to humanize the article," Bill explained. Before thinking about it Bill continued with, "You know include the little people," and then he corrected himself and said, "E-r-r, include civilians in the article."

Filer said, "Yeah I know what you mean. What about the next plot they want cleared?"

Bill added, "Go ahead and clear the next plot."

Filer hung up the CB and went back to sit with Wendy and Ed. "Cochrane agreed to the publicity photo," Filer told Wendy.

"Excellent," Wendy said. "We'll take the picture when we get back to the site."

Chapter 78

Later, back at the dig site, one of the grad students took several shots with a 35mm camera with a fancy lens. Filer continued a delicate excavation of the next area he and Ed had laid out. A full team of grad students were doing a careful excavation of the Fremont pit house remains in the previous site.

While he was running the Bobcat, Filer thought about the conversation he had with the students at his table. He had learned the students were working for minimum wages as part of a work study program. He was making twice the money they were making. Still he thought they were happier than he was to be scrabbling around in the dirt. His thoughts on this subject would stay with him for the rest of his career as a heavy equipment operator.

Bill surprised Filer when he arrived at the dig site. "Hey Filer," he said when Filer stopped the Bobcat beside his truck. "Today is your last day here. Dr. Jones told us Ed thinks he can run the Bobcat."

"Okay by me," Filer said hiding a little disappointment.

At the end of the work day Filer said good-bye to the students and drove back to his trailer.

Chapter 79

When he stepped inside the trailer he checked his answering machine. There weren't any messages. No one had called him from California. He grabbed a beer from the fridge and sat down in his easy chair. Girlfriend came into the living room and did her familiar cat stretch-front paws forward, forelegs flat to the floor and hind quarters raised. She opened her jaws and with a muted meow greeted Filer.

"Come on up," Filer invited her into his lap.

Girlfriend jumped up to his lap and repeated the cat stretch. Filer petted her.

Later, after cleaning-up, eating dinner and waiting for Girlfriend to come back into the trailer Filer was ready for a good night's sleep.

Filer had just closed his eyes when he heard a cry. Now he knew this couldn't be a coyote. It sounded like a human crying and it's coming from nearby; but the crying might be a coyote.

The next morning Filer was back on the D10 working with the loader to fill trucks with topsoil for the clean-up site.

At lunch Buddha asked Filer if he wanted to celebrate being back on the job with a beer after work.

For a moment Filer remembered the students' excitement and saw a little of that in Buddha's eyes.

"Sounds like a plan," Filer said.

For the rest of the day Filer pushed dirt and kept his attention on the arriving and departing trucks and the loader. The work took a lot more attention than operating the little Bobcat and he didn't have much time for philosophical thoughts.

Chapter 80

At the show-up Buddha told Filer to follow him to a casino in Winnemucca. Filer followed Buddha to the casino where they'd been before.

"What do you think of the local Indians," Buddha asked Filer?

"That site doesn't have anything to do with the local Indians," Filer said.

"What do you mean?"

"Well the Fremont culture dates back to the 1100's. They all disappeared in the 1200's.

"Is that so," Buddha said and smiled. "You're an expert huh?"

Filer looked a little uncomfortable and said, "I listened to Dr. Jones. She knows Indian history. I'm not talking about reservation stuff. These people were here before Europeans got here."

"You got all of this by keeping your ears open?"

"You know how it is. You have to pay attention."

Filer hesitated for a minute. "When I was a kid I had a hard time with reading and I had to listen to get what other kids got by reading. I finally got so I could read okay, but I still listen when someone is talking to me."

It was Buddha's turn to sit silent for a minute. "My sister's boy is autistic. He's probably worse off than you were. He can't sit in a classroom with normal kids. He has to have help. Life isn't always fair, so I'd say you beat down a disadvantage and came out on top. The funny thing is no one will ever give you the credit you deserve for that beat down."

Filer took a drink of his beer and nodded to Buddha. "I don't look at it like that. I was too busy raising hell," Filer smiled. "I was voted the most popular partier in my senior year. After school whatever was wrong never slowed me down making a living. Being color blind was harder because I couldn't pick the right color socks to match. So I bought black and white socks."

Buddha laughed. "What about stop lights?"

"I might be in trouble if they ever start putting red lights at the bottom and green lights on the top."

The two men drank their beers and both watched the crowd of people in the casino.

Just in a flash Filer thought he saw his next door neighbors. A cocktail waitress was being yelled at by a man. He yelled a little and sneaked a look around to see if any of the security people were watching. At the end of the yelling session the woman reached into her bra and handed the man money. He frowned and walked away from her to the 21 table.

As his attention was on the man the woman came to his table.

"Do you need beers?" she asked and tried to smile at Filer.

Filer looked at Buddha and he nodded, "Okay."

"Thanks Hon. We'll have another round."

"Who's she?" Buddha asked.

"She's my neighbor at the trailer park, but I don't know her. I think I got her mixed up with a coyote."

"She's pretty good looking for a coyote."

"I can see that," Filer agreed.

"Here she comes," Buddha said.

The neighbor put down two full beers and took away the two empties. Filer put an extra five dollars on her tray.

"Thanks," she said and really put together a smile.

Filer and Buddha took their beers to the dollar slots and played for a while until Filer said, "That's all for me. I'll see you at work tomorrow."

"Namaste," Buddha put his hands together and bowed his head toward Filer.

Chapter 81

At his trailer Filer went through the ritual of letting Girlfriend out for a quick roam around the trailer. She was supposed to be relieving herself. Girlfriend took her time and had a final roll in the dirt before she jumped up the steps and darted into the trailer.

"You're probably hungry now aren't you?"

Girlfriend curled around Filer's ankles and Filer narrowly avoided tripping over her while he opened a can of her favorite cat food and empty it into her bowl.

With his pet duties taken care of Filer checked his answering machine. No messages. His family in California was probably hanging out with the stars. They were being entertained without any help from him even though they wouldn't be there without the Mad Dog movie.

Later, Filer watched a TV variety show with Girlfriend curled up in his lap. He slept through the boring parts and maybe some of the interesting parts too.

Filer woke up after having dozed off and decided to go to bed when he heard a car door slamming. Then the neighbors slammed their way into their trailer. Before he made it into the bedroom he remembered the argument the two neighbors had in the casino.

"I guess they haven't made up yet," Filer thought.

Chapter 82

Only minutes later Filer hears the neighbors' trailer door slam. He didn't have time for another thought when there was a pounding on his door.

"What the hell?" Filer thought.

He got up from his easy chair and walked to the door. Girlfriend yawned and stretched out on the couch.

Filer opened the door not knowing what to expect and he still couldn't have been more surprised. The female next door neighbor was standing on his door step. The surprising element is that this attractive woman was standing in front of him topless, as in no shirt or bra.

"Please let me in before my boyfriend gets here."

Filer let the woman in and closed the door. He stood with her a minute before she looked at him with a lifted eyebrow and he took the hint and went into his bedroom and came back with one of his t-shirts and handed it to her.

"My name is Riley," said the half-naked neighbor. She took the T-shirt and pulled it over her head and bare chest. "Thanks for letting me in. If I can borrow your phone I'll call my sister and she'll come and get me."

"Yeah, sure," Filer said. He pointed to the telephone on the wall by the kitchen. "You should call the police."

The woman walked to the phone and called her sister. "Hi, Leslie I'm leaving him. We had a fight. I've had enough. He threw me out the door without a blouse. I'm at my next door neighbor's trailer. He loaned me a T-Shirt." She paused for a minute and then said, "You know

Richie. Any minute he'll be here banging on the door trying to get me to come back. But this time I'm not going back. I'm moving to Vegas."

She stopped talking and Filer assumed Riley was listening to her sister.

"Thanks Leslie. You're right I should have listened to you."

Riley hung up the phone and sat down on the couch. Girlfriend wound herself around Riley's ankle and Riley petted Girlfriend.

There was an uncomfortable silence in the small living room.

"You sure you don't want to call the police?"

"It wouldn't do any good. Are you married?"

"I am."

"I haven't seen your wife here."

"Here we go again," Filer thought. "My wife and daughter are in Hollywood."

"Really?"

"My daughter Kylie is one of the cast members of *American Daddy*."

Riley seemed to forget her circumstances for a minute. "I've seen that show. Is your daughter the young blond girl?"

"That's her."

"Oh my God, I can't believe it."

"Yeah it's hard to believe," Filer agreed.

"I saw you at the casino," Riley said. "I brought you two beers and you tipped me five dollars."

"It's a strategy to make new friends when you have to work in a lot of new towns. I started with Pegasus as a gold miner a month ago."

"I wish my boyfriend could get that kind of job."

"What's his problem?"

"He thinks he should be some kind of manager and he doesn't have a college degree and he has a really bad temper."

"It sounds like moving to Vegas is a good idea," Filer said.

"He wasn't too bad until we started living together."

Riley stopped petting Girlfriend and Filer noticed the cat stretch out its paws and kneed Riley's leg.

"Looks like you made a friend," Filer said and pointed to Girlfriend.

"I like animals. That's another problem. Richie doesn't like anything I like. That's another reason why I'm leaving him. He is jealous of everything I do that doesn't involve him."

"Do you want something to drink?" Filer offered.

Riley looked at him with a funny smile.

"I have water, coffee, tea or a beer."

"I could really use a glass of water."

Filer went to the kitchen and filled a glass with water from the tap.

"Thanks," Riley said.

Just when Riley started drinking the water they heard a horn honking outside.

"That's Leslie my sister." Riley sat the empty glass down and stood up giving Girlfriend a final stroke down her back.

"I'll return your T-shirt," Riley promised.

"That's all right I've got plenty of them."

"Just the same I'll get it back to you."

Filer opened the door for her and she stepped out of the trailer and walked to a blue Volkswagen Beetle her sister was driving.

"What's next?" Filer asked Girlfriend. "Probably missionaries, huh?"

With an interesting story to tell Filer called Abbey. Her phone rang several times and then gave him the answering machine message.

"Maybe next time," Filer thought.

Now it was really time to go to bed. He returned the water glass to the kitchen and placed it in the sink.

Chapter 83

In Hollywood Abbey listened to her husband's message. She was putting off calling him back. She told herself it was too late at night to call. She knew she had a responsibility to Filer and also a responsibility to her daughter. It was a decision she didn't want to make.

Chapter 84

At the show up Bill, the foreman took Filer aside. "I've got some good news and some bad news for you."

"I'll take the good news first."

"Okay, well you're back on the reclaim crew. And since we already have a dozer operator you're on as a truck driver."

"Nothing wrong with that," Filer said.

"That's not all. You'll be getting a fifty cent an hour raise."

Filer nodded.

"Now the bad news; once the reclaim is done Pegasus is closing down the Winnemucca operation and they'll be moving to a small town in Idaho. If you want to keep working for the company you'll have to move to Idaho. As I understand you're circumstances that'll put you even further away from your family."

Filer was silent.

"There is some good news in the bad news. The operation in Idaho is well established and if things go your way you can work there as long as you want. It would be a good way to put in your years until retirement. It might seem like a long time in the future now, but it isn't that long if you're going to start putting away some extra money for your retirement.

You have six months working here before you have to decide if you're going to move to Idaho." Bill paused for a minute and then said, "These big companies can be impersonal so you should know Cochrane has taken a liking to you."

The foreman delivered the crew to their work site.

Chapter 85

Filer had learned truck driving skills in Vietnam. Pegasus had some new trucks and some older ones. Generally new trucks meant driving them would be easier rather than harder. His truck was one he'd driven before so he only needed to get in the line-up and keep his place. He slipped in between Buddha and Chuy. His first day as a truck driver went by fast, a good omen. At the end of the day Bill picked up the crew and drove them back to the show up. He dropped the crew off and drove away.

"How about a beer?" Buddha asked.

"No, I can't. I've got to take care of Girlfriend. She'll be pissy if I don't let her out."

The rest of the crew looked at Filer.

"Don't get the wrong idea. My cat's name is Girlfriend."

"Yeah, okay sure," Chuy said and smiled.

Chapter 86

At his trailer Filer let Girlfriend out and checked his answering machine. No messages.

The neighbor's car wasn't in their driveway. The image of the attractive topless neighbor standing on his doorstep came back to Filer. He thought, "I'm a married man. I look but I don't touch."

The sound of tires crunching on gravel interrupted his thoughts and he just saw the rear end of the neighbors' vehicle pass by the front of his trailer.

A minute later, after the car stopped he heard a fist pounding on his front door.

"That's got to be Riley's boyfriend," Filer thought. "Okay Pard, you're asking for it." Filer went into the bedroom and got a .357 revolver out of the end table. He returned to the front door and opened it. The .357 was resting against his hip.

The boyfriend's angry scowl turned into a look of startled surprise.

"Uh, where is she?" he stuttered.

"Where's who?"

"My girlfriend."

"How would I know?" Filer answered in a flat tone.

"I know she came here yesterday."

"Not my circus, not my monkeys," Filer said not giving anything away. If the formerly angry boyfriend hadn't noticed it he raised the .357 slightly.

The boyfriend stood there with a gapping mouth and couldn't come up with anything to say. He tried to regain a little dignity by raising his hand, and then decided it would be better to just turn around and walk away.

Filer closed the door and sat down in his easy chair. "I guess we won't be having beers," he thought laying the .357 in his lap. When he calmed down he showered and put on a comfortable pair of Levis and a clean T-shirt.

"Just another day in the desert," Filer thought and put a TV dinner in the oven.

Chapter 87

Later, when the TV dinner was done Filer settled into his easy chair and couldn't help putting *American Daddy* on. He could see Kylie even if he wasn't getting any messages from her and Abbey.

American Daddy opened with a scene of the father character leering at Kylie while she sat chatting with his son. Just seeing the dad acting like a pervert put him off of the show so he switched channels and tuned into a re-run of *Law and Order*. He didn't last long and fell asleep in the first fifteen minutes of the program.

The sound of white noise static woke Filer up. Girlfriend was sprawled across his lap making soft cat snores.

Chapter 88

Following a quick breakfast the next morning Filer drove to the show up and parked. He was waiting for the foreman when Buddha and Chuy jumped into his pickup.

"Okay bro you've got to tell us about the sexy Professor you've been working for," Buddha insisted.

"Yeah," Chuy added. "I heard you're really into the Indian stuff now."

"You guys are jealous because I'm special and you're not."

"Huh," Buddha said.

"I got the sexy job because Cochrane knows I know how to act around educated people."

"So did you do the Professor or not?" Chuy asked.

"First of all I'm a happily married man. I know a lot of guys pick up a work site girlfriend first thing when they're hired for a new job. That's not my style."

"Okay so you didn't do the Prof. Did you learn anything being around the educated?"

He had two choices. Silence or talking about what he'd learned at the dig site. The stud code kicked in and the only option was to shut up and tough it out.

"What I know takes a lot of on the job experience or a semester at the University of Las Vegas. So you'll have to wait for the National Geographic special."

Buddha and Chuy knew Filer was pinned down with the Stud code so they laughed at Filer's attempt to side step their trap.

The Stud code was also the reason he didn't tell either of them about the topless neighbor. Maybe he'd tell them later.

Driving truck took Filer's mind off of Kylie and *American Daddy*. He didn't know what to think about Abbey's silence. This time the silence between them was longer than any time in the past. Was their relationship in trouble? It didn't seem fair that he worked to keep the two of them comfortable. No, that wasn't right. He was working to keep the family together and comfortable. Abbey had worked in the past. She had always worked during their marriage. This time was different. Now everything concerning the family was turned upside down. A final thought occurred before he lined up for a load. "What could he do about the family here in Nevada?" The only thing he could think of involved not sending money home. That would get Abbey's attention. Was it the right thing to do?

Driving the 777D Caterpillar truck required all of his attention around the loader. He was a rookie on this job even if he did know how to operate heavy equipment. People who didn't know what they were doing didn't last long.

"Okay Mad Dog, back her in and I'll load you out 'ole buddy'." This came over his truck radio.

It felt good to be a part of a team. Not family but close.

After work Filer stopped at a curio shop to find a seated Buddha for the dashboard of his truck. He thought it would be a homey touch. Inside the shop he saw several seated Buddha. And beside the seated Buddha he saw a statue of a seated woman. A sign said she was Guan Yin, a female Bodhisattva; the Chinese Goddess of Mercy. This small statue reminded Filer of Dyna Rees, so he bought her for his dashboard.

Filer received a written invitation inviting him and his family and friends to the opening of *Copper Thieves*.

With Cochrane's permission Filer made plans to attend the opening.

Chapter 89

The *Copper Thieves* movie would be opening in three hundred theaters. Filer and his guests were invited to the advance showing in Los Angeles where Shane owned an interest in a theater. His team would be conducting a poll to test an audience's interest in the film. If the film did well he would open the film in two hundred more theaters.

Shane had high hopes for his little independent film. It had heart and character as well as action and romance. His personal connection to the story had influenced his attitude toward the film as well. Filer Wilson had included Shane in the real life and work as a lineman. Line work, especially on high steel, was considered by some to be one of the world's most dangerous professions.

Shane had made a place for Filer in the making of *Copper Thieves* because of their friendship. He hoped Filer now had an appreciation of film making and his way of life. For the opening of the film Shane had written invitations for Filer, his family and his friends.

The theater for the opening was a classic of the golden age of theater construction. It had a grand lobby and concession stand. The auditorium had a main floor and an overhanging balcony.

Opening night Filer and Abbey arrived at the theater with Ozzie, his wife Trina, and Buddha. Rupert would be sitting with the cast and crew. Kylie came to the opening with Jeffery and the cast of *American Daddy*.

The opening wasn't a huge Hollywood event, but it was big enough. The press was interested and it would be written up. Shane, a producer and the lead actor, posed on a red carpet in front of the theater for photos. As the flash bulbs popped and people squinted at the star Shane spotted Filer and motioned him to come and stand with him. Filer stepped onto the red carpet alongside Rupert and Shane.

Filer had shaken hands with Pres. Johnson during his time in the Seabees; and he'd been to some company parties that got pretty wild. Now he was having that same kind of moment. With flashbulbs popping Filer wondered where his pictures would end up.

Shane smiled at Filer and shook his hand. "This is all part of the movie biz; not as scary as being up a pole huh?"

Filer smiled, "It's your game not mine."

"Let's go see a movie," Shane said.

They moved inside the Art Deco decorated lobby where people were being served wine and cheese.

"Where's the popcorn," Filer asked?

Shane said, "It's at the concession stand around the corner." Shane was used to Mad Dog down playing his reactions to everything Hollywood.

Shane glanced over Filer's shoulder and Filer turned in that direction. Kylie and the cast of *American Daddy* came around the corner talking, laughing and spilling popcorn on the lobby floor.

The *American Daddy* entourage spotted Filer and Abbey and headed their way.

"Be nice," Abbey said to Filer.

Relations between the lead star of *American Daddy* and Filer were at a low point. The way the director and stars on the show treated Kylie were better since Filer had sent Kylie to take lessons from Dyna, but the show was a long way from treating it's other female stars like human beings. Kylie kept telling Filer it was about fictional characters-Filer didn't believe it.

Larry, the star, was aware of Filer's dislike of him and the show. Off set Larry was as bad as his character was on the set. After Kylie used the training Dyna had given her Larry treated her with more respect. That didn't mean he had to treat anyone else respectfully. When the *American Daddy* group passed the *Copper Thieves* group Larry made the comment "Beware of the Mad Dog. Don't let him off his leash."

Larry smirked at Filer, "I saw your commercial; big guy like you being held down by a little girl. Some hero."

The group started to move away when Filer took Abbey's hand off his arm and stepped in front of Larry. "You don't want to find out why my nickname is Mad Dog. If you treat Kylie's character like a chippie I'm going to your place and kill you and everything around you old enough to die."

Larry looked puzzled for a minute and thought better of making a smart come back.

Shane moved to stand beside Filer and faced the *American Daddy* entourage. Kylie looked down and couldn't face Filer, and she continued standing with Jeffery.

For the moment Filer Mad Dog Wilson had the last word. The *American Daddy* cast moved past the *Copper Thieves* group and went into the theater auditorium.

"We'd better go in," Shane said.

Two rows of seats at the front of the auditorium were reserved for the critics. The next row was reserved for Shane and his party. Shane led his group down the aisle and ushered them into their seats. When everyone was seated he raised his hand to the projectionist room and the auditorium dimmed. Light rays that flickered through the air overhead produced images on the screen creating the picture title and credits flashing on the screen.

Chapter 90

Filer recognized the opening scene as if he were still there operating the county D10 many years ago. In the background he saw a stuntman fall off a pole that gave him his start as a lineman. He settled in his seat beside Abbey and gave his attention to the story on the screen.

When the last scene came onto the screen the audience sat quietly. Shane waited for a reaction. They could laugh, they could boo, and they could clap. Filer didn't have any money in the film but he waited as anxiously as Shane for the audience's reaction to the film.

When the audience started clapping for his picture Shane knew he had a money maker. The lights came up and Shane was shaking hands with people congratulating him on his success.

Chapter 91

Later, back at Shane's Malibu home Filer talked with Abbey in the carriage house.

They talked about divorcing. It wasn't an easy discussion. With her work as Kylie's manager and Kylie's money from her continuing role on *American Daddy* they could survive in Hollywood.

Their life assets and possessions would be either divided or sold and the money split between them.

When Filer left for Winnemucca he was leaving behind a big chunk of his life, but looking forward to what would come in the future. Now he would be chasing a livelihood that didn't include family life as he had come to know it. He had to find a new life.

Word got back to the Brotherhood that their man on the outside—the man they picked to do Steve Williams' errand would be rejoining them after he was convicted of attempted robbery and murder for hire.

Because of the hitman's failure Steve said his contract with the Brotherhood was void. When Steve decided not to give any more of his prison wages to the Brotherhood they no longer protected him and he was murdered by an inmate in another prison gang.

Cliff Williams was sent back to prison for violating the terms of his parole. The tattooed man testified that Cliff was a part of the murder for hire scheme to kill Filer Wilson.

The tattooed man got himself two more prison tattoos. On his left arm he had a coiled rattlesnake and on his right arm he had a tattoo of Wolfy leaping along his forearm.

Wolfy made a full recovery.

Chapter 92

After eight months with Pegasus in Winnemucca, two months more than he was promised, Pegasus closed its Winnemucca operation and transferred all the personnel willing to make the move to Soda Springs, Idaho.

Filer moved to Idaho and checked into a motel with Girlfriend. He hadn't yet gotten over the difficulty of parting with Abbey and Kylie. Filer and Abbey were divorced. Filer knew they weren't getting back together. Yet, as far as he could tell they weren't even angry with one another. They were parting on a friendly basis.

Abbey couldn't leave Kylie. Their bond was longer and stronger than Filer and hers. Filer understood.

When Pegasus closed in Nevada, Buddha and Chuy signed on with Pegasus Idaho in Soda Springs, Idaho.

The small town of Soda Springs didn't have more bars than churches; and Girlfriend wouldn't be bothered by coyotes.

Filer got out of the motel and moved into an apartment. So far it was a big improvement over his trailer.

On the job Filer became an ore train driver, using an off road tractor pulling three bottom dump trailers. It was a new experience for him.

It would take a while to make a life in the small town. It had been a long time since Filer had been a boomer chasing this kind of life style. He still preferred the bar scene to the church scene.

Two letters from California surprised Filer. The first letter came from Dyna Rees. Filer had become a favorite at her dojo when he returned to L.A. to take care of family business. Dyna included a small check for his last demonstration and exercise with the Dynamo Dojo for Women.

The second letter came from Kylie. Kylie was pregnant. The director of *American Daddy* figured out a way to make her pregnancy a part of the program. In six months Filer would be a grandfather. Filer smiled, pleased that Kylie still wanted him in her world.

Girlfriend jumped into Filer's lap between him and the letter. She wanted all of Filer's attention. Filer petted her and raised the letter so he could finish reading it.

Kylie and Abbey had moved out of Shane's carriage house into their own apartment. Kylie gave Filer her new address and phone number. She signed her letter-Love ya Dad, Kylie.

"That's L.A. and I'm here in Idaho," Filer thought. "Well Kitty, I'm going to see what's happening here in Idaho."

Chapter 93

Filer got dressed and drove to Main Street and the Stockman's Bar.

From just inside the dark entrance way Filer saw a pool table. On the wall beside the pool table a reproduction of Van Goth's Night Café was hanging. Taking a couple of steps farther inside he took in a back room where a darts player, surrounded by other darts players threw darts at a dart board.

He took a stool at the bar where a nice looking young woman was working as the bartender.

"What are you drinking," the bartender asked in a friendly tone?

"Give me a Bud, darlin'," Filer said and gave the woman a Mad Dog smile from the boomer days.

"It's Hoops." Hoops answered Filer, and smiled back.

"Step number one," Filer thought, "You've got to get to know people."

"I haven't seen you before."

"No you haven't. I just moved here. I'm driving for Pegasus."

One of two women sitting at a table raised an empty glass gesturing to the bartender.

"Excuse me," the bartender said to Filer.

She poured two drinks and left the bar taking the drinks to the two women. When she got back behind the bar she said, "My friends want to know who the tall bearded stranger is?"

Filer turned and smiled the Mad Dog boomer smile at the two ladies. He raised his beer to them and said to Hoops, "Their next drinks are on me."

"Good move," Hoops said, "they're my friends Sugar and Surfer Girl. They work next door at the Main Street Café. Sugar is a damn good cook and Surfer Girl is a fine waitress. If you get in good with them you get in good with a lot of other people including me."

"Sounds like good advice," Filer said.

Filer drank his beer and listened to the tavern noises around him; the darters at their board, the women talking at their table and a song on the juke box playing. "All part of the puzzle," he thought to himself. "If he stayed long enough it would be a puzzle he would become a part of."

Filer was ready to leave the bar when the door opened and Chuy and Buddha came in. They walked to the bar and took stools on either side of him.

"Haven't you ever heard you're not supposed to drink alone," Buddha says.

"That's why I'm here," Filer answered.

"Who's your friend?" Buddha motioned to the bartender.

"This is Hoops."

Hoops heard her name and came to stand in front of them.

"Hoops, this is Buddha and Chuy. We worked together in Nevada."

"Welcome gentlemen," Hoops said.

Buddha ordered another round of beers and Filer was there for another round before he could leave.

After finishing his second beer he left Hoops three two dollar bills for a tip. "Step number two-give her something to remember him by," Filer said to himself smiling.

"See you later," Filer gave a little salute to Buddha and Chuy.

"That's right, you have to get home to Girlfriend," Buddha said.

Hoops looked disappointed.

Buddha saw the look. "Don't worry that's his cat's name."

When he got back to his apartment Filer talked to Girlfriend, "We're not alone Girlfriend. We know Buddha and Chuy and some new friends in town."

Girlfriend didn't say anything, but she purred in agreement to her big friend.

THE END

Acknowledgement

Any work of fiction is an accumulation of elements. Tall tales, bits of business, fictionalized life stories and narrative are all used to make the sum greater than its parts.

So, a novel is a puzzle to be put together from its various pieces. The pieces of the puzzle are discovered, identified and developed by the author or authors.

Mad Dog Goes to Hollywood is a work of fiction assembled and developed from its parts by myself and Everett 'Mad Dog' Perry. The tall tales, and fictionalized life stories come from the real life experiences of Everett 'Mad Dog' Perry. The bits of business and narrative connecting the novel are my contribution.

Other persons helping to put this puzzle together include the staff of Soda Springs Public Library, May Alvarez my project coordinator at iUniverse, Brianna at Staples, who was very patient making proofs to be corrected; and last but not least Kristie 'Hoops' Newman. Kristie rivaled Spell Check in making me feel humble as to my ability to proof read my own work.

For those who have gone through the process of writing and eventually completing a novel, the assistance of others who are willing to read, re-read and read again a manuscript cannot be overestimated. Thanks to all persons above who suffered/enjoyed the process of putting together the puzzle that became *Mad Dog Goes to Hollywood*.